Everybody Deserves One Good Day

Hugh Gillespie

For
Pupils and Teachers
of
Possilpark

British Library Cataloguing in Publication Data

ISBN 0 340 63913 X

First published 1995
Impression Number 10 9 8 7 6 5 4 3 2 1
Year 1999 1998 1997 1996 1995

Typeset by Wearset, Boldon, Tyne and Wear.
Printed in Great Britain for Hodder & Stoughton Educational, a division of Hodder Headline Plc, 338 Euston Road, London NW1 3BH by
Cox & Wyman Ltd, Reading.

CHAPTER

Sixty-three. 63. Not a particularly large number. Not as great as 472. 472 Paladin Street. Today, however, sixty-three steps *seemed* like climbing a mountain to Joanne. Her breathing was shallow. Her legs were not responding to the frantic signals from her brain. Get a move on! She was experiencing an unwelcome sensation of warm liquid streaming down the small of her back. Joanne had no time to consider whether this was the result of her present exertions or of lingering in the rain outside her favourite shop. Probably both.

The walls of the close were weeping. Condensation caused the surface to feel moist beneath her hand as she gathered herself for the final assault on the summit. At least the dampness would drown the pong of Old Granny Stewart's army of cats. Joanne wondered whether the long-awaited renovation would mean she could sit out on a dry stair. Escape to the landing, away from the babble. What was she saying? Soon she would have a room of her own.

For a brief moment Joanne contemplated the bliss of privacy. She would not be catapulted out of her dreams by the blaring tone of Jackie's ghetto-blaster. She would not have to pick her way through Jackie's discarded clothing to reach the door. She would not be encouraged to sit in the kitchen, watching mindless television programmes, whenever Jackie 'had private matters to discuss' with the 'gorgeous' Sean.

No. Soon, she would be able to put up her own posters. She would have a wardrobe to herself. She could invite Sara to listen to some records one evening (if she ever managed to get a hi-fi). Maybe even sleep over! And, most important of all, there would be plenty of space for the bike.

Joanne reached the front door. 'GORDON'. It seemed strange to Joanne, even after two years. She still thought of herself as Joanne McCallum. The school register listed her as Gordon. Her dinner ticket stated Gordon. James had even gone so far as to have Gordon lettered on his new tracksuit top. But she would always be McCallum.

Before placing the key in the lock Joanne pulled the catalogue from her carrier bag. She gazed longingly at the glossy photographs, pored over each convincing description, cherished the thrill of ownership. Rapid calculations brought her back to earth. Where would she ever find the money?

Joanne thrust her precious brochure deep into her bag. Sixty-three was not, it was true, a particularly large number. Sometimes, however, five could seem too many. This was uppermost in Joanne's mind as she pushed the door open.

'Is that you, Joanne?' came a voice from the kitchen. 'You're late. Where have you been?' Mrs. Gordon's tone was that curious mix of anger and concern mothers reserve for such occasions.

As Joanne stepped into the Gordon kitchen her nostrils were assailed by a battery of scents and smells. Her mother stood at the cooker stirring the ingredients of the wok. The spicy aroma tickled Joanne's palate.

An earthy smell of grass and soil, dislodged from James's football boots, emanated from in front of the fireplace. He crouched, his long legs tucked uncomfortably under him, furiously rubbing at one boot. He didn't look up when his sister entered.

The most unusual combination of smells hung over the room's other inhabitant. The cloying odour of warm milk, the fragrance of talcum powder and the rank stink of a disposable nappy (yet to be disposed) could only mean that Steven McNab Gordon was ensconced in his bouncy chair, surveying his kingdom. His bright, blue eyes fixed Joanne as she dripped on to his mat. In spite of herself she smiled.

'Where have you been?' her mother repeated,

inspecting her younger daughter. 'You look like a drowned rat.'

'A drowned whale, more like,' sneered James, temporarily abandoning his polishing, to participate in his second favourite hobby.

Fire flashed in Joanne's eyes. Just wait, James McCallum-Gordon!

'I'm sorry, mum. I walked Sara home,' Joanne lied. It was only a small lie.

'That must be some sight,' interrupted James, 'Laurel and Hardy. Eh, Ollie?'

Margaret Gordon sensed her daughter's pain. Joanne was certainly overweight. She seemed to have gained more than a few pounds over the last year. Mrs. Gordon had hardly had time to notice. Steven occupied much of her time. Most of it, according to Jackie the other night.

Ian being away didn't help, of course. Still, the rigs paid good money and they would need all the money they could lay their hands on for the renovation. They had talked about it, argued about it for a long time before reaching their decision. It was a waste of his talent, she had said. He could be a chef in any number of hotels in and around Glasgow. The oil rig workers demanded quality catering, he had replied. And besides the money. . . .

Always the money. If the baby was just a bit older,

Margaret thought, she could ask her mum to look after him. She could then work part-time. No shortage of jobs for someone with her experience in word-processing. Her mum didn't fancy babies at this stage in their development.

'Too messy!' she had exclaimed more than once. 'I couldn't stand you and I couldn't stand your brother Robert. All those dirty nappies! No, I've done my stint. Send them to me when they're house-trained, thank you very much.'

Steven was messy. And he girned to be lifted. And he woke the household every single night. But he also lit up the room with his gurgling laugh. James talked of nothing but football and the Rangers, which weren't quite the same thing. But he was brimming with enthusiasm. And he would someday be Scotland's midfield dynamo, whatever that was. Jackie used the house as a hotel. She breezed in and breezed out again. On occasion, lately, she stormed out. Margaret recognised herself in this strong-willed young woman. Joanne was . . . fat. Plump, if one was being kind. And often recently she appeared lost in thoughts which she didn't choose to share. It was her age, her mother hoped.

'Don't take that jacket off.' Mrs. Gordon ordered, as Joanne struggled to peel an arm out of a sodden sleeve. 'I need you to go a few messages for me.

There's a list on the mantelpiece. You'll get them all at the Co-op.'

'But, mum, I'm soaked through. Why can't Maradona here go?' Joanne moaned. The Argentinian was the only footballer Joanne could identify. James had twenty-four pictures of him above his bed.

James beamed at his sister's unwitting compliment. 'Because I've got my papers to do and then I'm off to my training.'

'And you've to feed that rabbit,' his mother reminded him.

'And I've to feed Moby,' agreed James. 'Anyway you could use the exercise, Slim.'

'That's enough, James.' Mrs. Gordon felt obliged to step in. James would, she knew, take on the toughest bully in the street to defend his sister but at home he failed to see the harmful effect his joking had on Joanne. 'You tidy up this mess and get about your business.'

Joanne realised that there was little point in arguing the matter further. Besides, she had no wish to get into her mother's bad books. Indeed, she needed to be sure she was in a good mood before asking the big question. Wiping a damp strand of hair off her forehead she retrieved the shopping list from the mantelpiece. She lifted the small red purse containing the money she would require.

Perhaps the shopping expedition would allow her time to plan her approach to her mum. How could she introduce the subject? How could she persuade her that this meant the world to her? That it would be an invaluable purchase? It would take her out from under her mother's feet. It would get her fit. It would. . . .

'Jo-Jo, want to know how to get rid of twenty pounds of unsightly fat?' James shouted as she opened the front door.

Joanne was startled out of her rehearsal.

'Cut off your head!' cackled the voice from the kitchen.

A tear escaped as Joanne hurtled down sixty-three steps.

CHAPTER

Timing is everything. Helping her mother wash the dishes provided the ideal opportunity to broach the subject. Catch her in a good mood. When her defences are down. Whatever, thought Joanne.

Joanne had suffered inwardly throughout the first course as James continued to make her the butt of his jokes. She had tolerated each jibe about her size without once losing her temper. Eventually Mrs. Gordon had intervened, forbidding her son to insult his sister further, and instructing him to finish eating his meal in silence.

Margaret Gordon had marvelled at her daughter's restraint. Last week Joanne had hurled a football boot at James for his insensitive comments.

'I thought there was an eclipse of the sun,' he had sneered, 'until I realised Joanne was standing at the window.'

During the second course, Pear Belle Helene, Jackie had come in from her work. Ian had revolutionised the family meals, much to Joanne's delight. This dessert of pears, ice cream and rich, dark chocolate afforded her especial pleasure. This evening Joanne's enjoyment was somewhat spoiled by having to listen to her sister's incessant yapping about the shop.

'You should have seen the state of this customer. . . .'

'Marie sold £200 worth of clothing to this guy and his wife. . . .'

'You want to see the fabulous leather jacket we just got in. . . .'

Only the fact that Sean, the light of her life, was meeting her in less than an hour dragged Jackie away from the table. Instead she barricaded herself in the bathroom for thirty minutes, 'making herself beautiful'. When she emerged James stated he didn't notice any improvement.

Now, both Jackie and James had gone. James, kitted out in his club tracksuit, had jogged to his football training. Jackie, resplendent in the latest fashion (courtesy of her discount), had sauntered to the bus stop to embrace her patient boyfriend.

Mrs. Gordon washed; Joanne dried and put away. Steven sat in his chair anticipating the fun of bathtime to follow. First the dishes, then the baby.

'Mum, can I ask you something?' began Joanne,

trying to sound as casual as possible. 'Something important.'

'Can I stop you?' Margaret Gordon said, appearing engrossed by the pile of dishes, stacked ready to be cleaned.

Joanne hesitated. Oh well, here goes, in for a penny, as Nana would say. 'You know that bike shop, "Deals on Wheels", at the corner of Ottoman Street, next to the chippy? . . .'

Her mother grunted, hoping her daughter would get to the point. And soon.

'Well, you know the man in it, Mr. Ross. Well, he gave me a catalogue with all the bikes in it. To look at. And there was this one bike, one of these new mountain bikes, like Sara's mum and dad bought her. Well, not quite the same. This one was pink, "Hot Pink Vapour" it was called, and I was just wondering. . . .'

Mrs. Gordon halted Joanne in full flow. 'You were just wondering if you could get one,' she concluded her daughter's long-winded approach.

Joanne exhaled. 'Well, yes,' she answered feebly.

'Of course you can. As long as its not too expensive,' Mrs. Gordon said.

'Mr. Ross gave me all the details,' Joanne got going again. 'It's only £250 and that includes a water bottle and a helmet and. . . .'

'Hold your horses a minute,' her mum commanded. 'Only £250! That's a fortune!'

Joanne's face fell.

'But I'm not saying no right away,' Margaret continued. 'I'll have to discuss it with Ian first but I think we can work something out.'

Like the sun emerging from behind a cloud, Joanne's face glowed. Had she not been holding two dinner plates at the time she would have cartwheeled across the room. If there had been space. If she could have executed such a strenuous feat. The plates excused her.

'Of course, you understand this bike would be a joint Christmas and birthday present. It wouldn't be fair to James, or Jackie for that matter, if you got a big present and they had to make do with their usual.'

A tiny grain of apprehension seeded itself in Joanne's mind. It flourished. 'But when would I get the bike?' she blurted out.

'Oh don't worry, we'd give you it at Christmas. We wouldn't ask you to wait till February,' her mother assured her.

'Christmas!' Joanne exploded, 'Christmas! That's seven months away! I thought you meant I could get it now. You know, with that money you got from your work.'

Mrs. Gordon stared at her not-so-wee girl. She was

taken aback by the force of her outburst. Jackie and she fought like cat and dog at times. Her eldest child was no longer a child. She needed breathing space. James was irrepressible in his efforts to be the life and soul of the party. He was like a joke novelty from Tam Shepherd's; he amused and annoyed at the same time. The walking whoopee cushion.

Joanne, however, was placid and reliable. She wasn't one to make a fuss. She wasn't in the habit of asking for things. Perhaps, Margaret considered, she had paid too little attention to her younger daughter recently. She was at a difficult age. Were there any easy ages?

'James is off to Italy with the boys' club, Jackie's flying off to Benidorm with Sean, and I'll be stuck here all summer . . .' Joanne whined.

'In the company of your boring mother, I know,' Mrs. Gordon interrupted, 'but let's get a few things straight. Firstly, James has saved the money from his paper run to afford the trip to Italy. Except to play football he's hardly been over the door for the last two months.'

Grudgingly Joanne nodded her agreement.

'Secondly,' her mother went on, 'Jackie is working. She deserves to get a break from this place.'

From Jackie's account of her day Joanne never got the impression that her sister particularly exerted herself. She scowled at her mother's singular testimonial.

'And thirdly, young lady,' she said, 'the money I received from the tax people is earmarked for a pram for Steven. He's only got that old buggy and it's on its last legs.' Margaret was aware of the ludicrousness of this final statement even as she voiced it. She hoped Joanne wouldn't notice.

Without intending to, both females turned to gaze at the child in question. The entire debate had passed over his head. In all senses. He smiled his most beguiling smile. Joanne steeled herself to resist.

'Oh yeah,' she retorted, deliberately becoming sloppy in her speech, 'let's go out and buy yet another present for the spoiled brat.'

'Joanne McCallum!' her mum shouted. As she said it Margaret knew she had inadvertently turned the spotlight on the subject both mother and daughter would have preferred to remain in the dark.

Joanne placed her dish-towel on the draining board. Without a word she walked out of the kitchen, shutting the door behind her.

Margaret Gordon sat down. She listened to the front door closing and her daughter's footsteps on the stairs. She thought back to the break-up. How can you expect a child to understand when the adults involved can't explain what went wrong?

Steven started to bawl.

CHAPTER

Saint Mungo's Hill was situated at the most westerly point of Northwood. A narrow ribbon of residential houses, it acted as the boundary marker between the old established tenements of Northwood proper and the giant housing scheme of Whitechurch thrown up after the last war.

The inhabitants of the Hill, as it was popularly known, worked in banks, offices, schools or colleges. Some ran their own small businesses. Sara's father was an architect in a firm near Charing Cross.

The majority of the children from the Hill either attended one of the private schools in the town or travelled by bus to Castleton Academy just outside Glasgow, in Castle Fergus. A twenty-minute journey, twice a day, was preferable, their parents believed, to subjecting their offspring to the hazards of Northwood Secondary. Few, if any, of these concerned parents had stepped foot inside either school before making this decision.

Sara Devlin trusted her mum and dad to enrol her

in Northwood. One or two classmates, who didn't know any better, delighted in 'slagging' her. To them she was a 'snob' to be mercilessly baited. Sara had learned to cope with their stupidity. She was sufficiently mature to realise that the difference in their social status was a mere accident of birth.

She enjoyed Miss Martin's class. The teacher endeavoured to make her lessons and projects interesting. Occasionally her enthusiasm resulted in chaos. The attempt to build a life-size whale in the gym had floundered amid reams of paper, glue, struts of wood and a group of boys determined to have a carry-on. Even Sara's father had admitted that it had looked good at the design stage.

Sara was surprised to hear her dad downstairs, opening the door to her friend Joanne. Surprised but glad. Without taking her eyes from the monitor she called to her pal.

'I'm up here playing, sorry, working at the computer. Come on up.'

'You are being summoned to the Royal Chamber, Josie,' George Devlin said, grinning.

Joanne liked this burly man. He was like a big kid, open and playful. She had, after initial reluctance, appreciated the significance of having a pet name bestowed upon her. The Devlins always made her feel at ease in their home.

'Don't look so glum,' he added, noticing the morose expression on Joanne's face, 'or I won't let you help me demolish the chocolate gateau Liz made this afternoon. We can get fat together, eh, Josie?'

Sara's father was the only person whom Joanne allowed to kid her about this touchy subject. This was because he was only too ready to crack jokes about his own weight problem.

'I'm exactly the right weight for a man of my height,' he'd say. 'Nine foot four!'

Sara's bedroom showed a precision her father would have approved. Tidiness was an art form. A place for everything and everything in its place. Nana Livingstone's saying sprang to mind whenever Joanne entered her friend's room.

A cursory glance was sufficient to establish that Sara's parents were comfortably off. They had bestowed all manner of 'hi-tech' goods on their only child. In addition to the computer she possessed her own television and hi-fi. The decor also reflected luxury unknown to Joanne. Curtains, cushions and quilt cover matched; an abstract swirl of grey, red and black, selected by Sara and 'made up' by a woman her mother employed for such purposes.

Joanne did not envy her friend. Not even where the mountain bike was concerned. She perceived an emptiness in Sara's life which all the treasures in Aladdin's cave could not fill.

'Well,' Sara said, unable to keep her curiosity concealed, 'how did you get on?'

'Don't ask,' Joanne muttered, before proceeding to blurt out the whole sorry tale. When she had finished her friend commiserated with her.

'Look, Joanne, you know you're welcome to use my bike whenever you wish.'

'That's not the point, Sara,' Joanne replied, rather more testily than she had intended. 'I want a bike of my own. And not just for the stupid cycling proficiency test either. I'd probably fail that anyway.'

'For goodness sake, stop feeling so sorry for yourself,' Sara rebuked. 'You're the one who's always telling me to have more confidence, to look on the bright side.'

'Aye, I know, every cloud has a silver lining and all that rubbish. But as I was trying to say . . .'

'Before you were so rudely interrupted . . .'

'Before I was so rudely interrupted . . . the first time,' Joanne continued, a lighter tone in her voice, 'she doesn't understand what the bike means to me. James has his daft football team. Jackie has the "gorgeous" Sean . . .'

'Twisted round her little finger . . .'

'And she has Prince Steven of Northwood, the

world's most perfect baby.' A hint of bitterness had returned to Joanne's voice. 'Honestly, Sara, I'm the invisible girl in that house.'

Her friend exploded with laughter. Sara observed the miserable Joanne shifting her bulk on the bed. A flush appeared on the larger girl's face, a blend of annoyance and embarrassment.

'Not you too, Sara,' she chided. 'I get enough cracks about my size at home. You're my pal. You're supposed to be sensitive, to respect my feelings, and all that.'

'I do, I do,' insisted Sara, trying to recover her composure. 'How's the new diet going? Lost any weight?'

Joanne looked sheepish. She had attempted several times to shake off a few pounds. Without success. Food held a peculiar fascination for her.

'And that's another thing,' she said, evading the issue, 'a bike would help. Think of the exercise. All those hills.'

'To be fair, Joanne, your mum's probably right. Steven can't go about in that ramshackle old pushchair much longer.'

It was Joanne's turn to explode. With anger. 'Steven this, Steven that! I'm sick of hearing the wee pig's name. To listen to my mother you'd think the sun shone out of his. . . .'

'Joanne! Calm down. Be reasonable.'

'Reasonable! Is it unreasonable to ask for a bike?' Joanne demanded.

'But your mum promised you a bike for Christmas.'

'Christmas, as I keep telling folk, is seven months from now!' Joanne continued her rant. 'It's alright for you to make your pronouncements, Sara Devlin. You only have to sigh and your mummy comes running with the catalogue.'

As soon as the words escaped her lips Joanne regretted them. She stared at the pattern on the rug rather than meet her friend's eye.

'I would exchange everything in this room, Joanne, for a brother,' Sara whispered, 'even one like your James.'

Joanne raised her head to discover a tear slowly rolling down her friend's cheek. At that instant she wished the earth would swallow her up.

'Sara, I'm sorry. I didn't mean what I said. I just get so angry and I lash out at anything and everything. Please forgive me.'

Sara laid a hand on her friend's arm. In the same tremulous tone as before, she spoke.

'Can you keep a secret, Joanne? I'm sorry, of course you can. Well, I had a brother. My twin, Kenneth. I was the first one born. Twenty minutes older than Kenneth. My dad said once that Kenneth got the looks and I got the brains. Anyway, this was before we moved here, when we lived in the Southside.'

Joanne was about to ask a question but the intense expression on Sara's face warned her off. Questions could wait.

'As you can imagine, my mother doted on her two babies. She paraded us everywhere. To all the aunties. To the grandparents. Everywhere. Kenneth and Sara, the heavenly twins.

'One night we were bathed and put to bed. We slept at either end of the same cot. In the morning Kenneth was dead. I was cooing and giggling. And he was dead. My dad told me all this years later, of course. "Cot Death", like you read in the papers. It's got some big fancy name, a syndrome or something.

'Soon after, we moved here. My mum never mentions him. All our baby photos are locked away somewhere. It's as if he never existed.'

'Oh, Sara, I really am sorry. I had no idea,' Joanne said gently. 'All the times I've moaned about James and the baby. . . .'

Sara squeezed her friend's hand. Joanne felt a tremor, a very slight quaking, pass through the other girl's body. Both girls sat for a few minutes, neither knowing what to say.

Eventually Sara broke the silence. 'Perhaps you

can understand why my mum treats me as if I'm some kind of china doll. Why I'm never allowed out late. Why they spoil me rotten. Do you think I enjoy being wrapped up in cotton wool?'

Joanne took both Sara's hands in hers. They shared a common bond. She knew their friendship would be stronger now.

There was a knock on the door. George Devlin stuck his head round. The sense of stillness alerted him that something was up. He registered this but said nothing. If his daughter wished him to know she would tell him in her own good time.

'Hi, you two. Thought you might care to join me in demolishing this gateau.' From behind the door he produced the most sumptuous cake Joanne had ever seen. It was three layers deep, covered in the thickest dark chocolate icing, and topped with whipped cream.

Joanne recalled her resolution. 'Thanks, Mr. Devlin, but. . . .'

Sara nudged her friend.

'Oh, alright. Maybe just a small piece. . . .'

CHAPTER

The Town. No matter how frequently or how prominently they promoted the notion of Glasgow as a city, to the natives it would remain the Town. European City of Culture. Before that, Garden Festival City of Great Britain. Exotic flora and Italian tenors had long since departed, leaving the ordinary Glaswegian, if such a creature existed, to contemplate the reality of Saturday shopping in Argyle Street. Miles Better!

Like ants at a picnic they descended on the town, swarming, scavenging, retreating to their bolt-holes with their pickings. This Saturday Margaret Gordon, daughter Joanne and baby Steven had enlisted in the invading army. They would besiege the department stores in search of loot. In this instance, one luxury pram to transport the newest recruit to the Gordon regiment.

Margaret had drawn up a plan of campaign. They would begin at Fraser's. She had chosen Jackie's pram there. A beautiful Marmet, it had served Jackie, then

James, and finally, Joanne. She should never have given it away to Susan. Ah, but she had no intention of having any more kids, did she?

They drew a blank at Fraser's. 'I'm sorry we no longer have a Nursery Department,' the young sales assistant informed her. Margaret looked downcast. It was going to be a long day, thought Joanne.

Joanne had been given the task of pushing the baby-buggy. After yesterday's argument she had tried to stay out of her mother's way. When she returned from Sara's she had gone straight to bed. No supper and no goodnight kiss. She hadn't minded missing out on a soppy kiss but the supper had been a sacrifice. Still, her mother needed to appreciate that children had a right to be upset, too.

Manoeuvring the buggy proved a tricky business. Twice she clipped the heels of other shoppers. Serves them right for dawdling! Once she collided with the concrete base of a litter-bin. Stupid place to put it! Who uses them anyway? The accumulated debris of wrappers, pokes and cartons couldn't come up with an answer.

All the way down Buchanan Street Steven beamed at passers-by. Instinctively they responded in kind, their faces wearing the most outrageous grins. Joanne felt even more ignored.

Crossing Argyle Street was hazardous. A

continuous convoy of buses blocked their path. Single-deckers, double-deckers, Kelvin buses, 'Corpy' buses and an assortment of private buses formed an almost impenetrable wall. To be strictly accurate, there were no Corporation buses; there was no longer a Corporation. We have a District Council, part of a Regional Council, but we miss the comfort of the old Corporation. Glasgow would always be bigger than Strathclyde.

A supporters' bus, full of optimistic faces, inched past. Margaret enjoyed a quiet smile. In this notoriously divided city the buses were orange. Previously they had been green, white and gold. Nobody bothered.

The Saint Enoch Centre glistened in the sunlight. It was an impressive sight, its enormous glass roof shining like a beacon. Following the monstrosity of the S.E.C.C. this was a welcome addition to the New Glasgow.

'Can we go on the subway?' Joanne asked, immediately regretting she had spoken. She had been determined not to ask her mother for anything ever again. The giant orange U overhead had prompted this careless lapse. 'Steven has never gone on the subway before . . .' she added, trying to regain her previous composure.

Mrs. Gordon laughed. She knew how much delight

her daughter took in travelling on Glasgow's toytown underground system. The Clockwork Orange. 'Maybe later, if we get all our shopping,' she replied. She sensed a slight thaw.

The centre was packed with shoppers. Margaret wanted to check out two stores, at opposite ends of the complex. The first was a disappointment. Push-chairs, buggies and carry-cots in abundance but no real prams. It seemed she wanted the Q.E.2 and they only built ferries nowadays.

'Joanne, wait about here with Steven while I go to Mothercare.'

Joanne was pleased to avoid the mass of humanity thronged between here and the far end. As soon as her mum was swallowed up by the crowd she wheeled her beloved brother towards the escalator. Let her mother find her!

Mothercare offered greater variety. Only Margaret discovered they didn't sell prams: they sold 'baby transport systems'. Nothing on display appealed to her. Everything was designed for 'flexibility' according to the assistant. Nobody seemed to value the sheer style of the traditional pram, she felt.

'We do have one pram in our catalogue which might fit the bill,' she said. 'It comes in at about £250.'

Margaret studied the information in the glossy booklet. The body, chassis and canopy were sold separately. From the picture it certainly appeared substantial enough. It wasn't quite what she was looking for, but. . . .

'It's lovely,' she admitted, 'but I'd like to think it over, thanks.'

'Of course,' agreed the saleswoman. 'It's a big decision. Here, take this with you and have a good read at home.' She thrust the catalogue into Margaret's hand. 'Hope you don't mind me asking, is this your first?'

Margaret wasn't sure whether this was a genuine inquiry or part of the sales patter. She blushed. Secretly, she was flattered. 'I sometimes wish it was,' she answered.

Pausing only to steal a glance at her reflection in a plate-glass window she hurried off to rejoin her children.

They were nowhere to be seen.

Margaret experienced a moment of panic. She shuddered, pushing away her worst fears. Keep calm. Think. Where would Joanne go? She headed for the escalator to the upper level.

She spied her errant offspring before they noticed her presence. They were at the ice-rink. Through the moving horde of shoppers she glimpsed Joanne hunched down beside the buggy. She was pointing towards the skaters, providing Steven with a running commentary on the action. Both parties seemed very animated.

'I thought I . . .' began Mrs. Gordon, then changed her mind. 'I thought I would find you two here. Enjoying yourselves?' She curled her arm affectionately round Joanne's waist, playfully squeezing a roll of fat.

'I was just showing Steven the ice skaters. Telling him I'd bring him here when he was a big boy, wasn't I?'

The baby drooled down the front of his jacket.

Mother and daughter looked at each other. The ice had melted. Joanne pressed her hand into her mum's to seal the reconciliation.

'Why don't I leave the pair of you here a bit longer while I go across to Arnott's? I'll give you some money and you can buy something to eat from one of the stalls.' She indicated a row of counters offering dishes to suit all tastes: hamburgers, tacos, fish suppers, chow mein, stovies. 'Sit at a table and don't move till I get back.'

Joanne had the sneaking suspicion that she was being bribed. Casting her eyes down the first of several menus she didn't much mind.

On the second floor of Arnott's Margaret Gordon found her dream pram. A de-luxe model Silver Cross. The price tag said £350. That would put paid to almost the entire amount she had received in the tax rebate. But it was an exquisite machine. A thing of beauty.

Steven deserved this masterpiece of engineering. She deserved it! So Margaret Gordon tried to convince herself. She had promised herself that this baby, this adorable and adored baby, would receive the best she could afford. No hand-me-downs. No cheap versions of superior brands. This was her latest and last child.

Then she thought of Joanne. She was to have been the completion of her family. Before things had gone wrong. Before John had left. Before she had met Ian. Joanne had been her baby.

'Hello, love, did you have something nice to eat?' Margaret greeted her daughter with a warm smile.

'Cracking!' Joanne answered. 'I had a cheeseburger. And a portion of French fries, you know, chips. And a Coke, medium size. Or maybe it was a Pepsi? No, it was definitely a Coke. And . . .'

'Enough!' interrupted her mother, marvelling at her daughter's pleasure in eating.

'And I fed Steven a rusk from the bag,' Joanne finished. She scanned her mum's face for approval. It must be windy outside. Her mother's eyes were watery.

Mrs. Gordon gazed fondly at Joanne and her charge. 'Well,' she said, 'I'm just going back to

Mothercare to order the bold boy's pram and when I come back we're off to Greaves' to buy you a new tracksuit, young lady.'

Joanne would have preferred a shell-suit like Sara's. A 'bomb-suit' Mrs. Devlin had called it. Still, the tracksuit was unexpected. Never look a gift horse in the mouth, as her Nana would say. Okay, so it wasn't a mountain bike but. . . .

'Thanks, mum,' she said and surprised Margaret Gordon by hugging her until she could scarcely breathe.

CHAPTER

Before she had even turned the big key in the lock Joanne heard the scurrying of a small animal. She prayed that it was Moby. The old washhouse was spooky at the best of times without encountering mice or rats. Creepy-crawlies she could just about cope with, but creatures with long tails. . . .

The heavy wooden door jolted suddenly. Joanne found herself pitched into the dank gloom. She threw her arms out to cushion her fall. Her fingers slithered on the slimy surface of the floor. Her knees, protected by her new tracksuit trousers, seemed to have landed in some unknown mushy substance. Mushy and smelly.

Joanne raised her head. Two large pink eyes stared unblinkingly at her. As she became accustomed to the dimness of the washhouse she could make out a set of powerful white teeth.

A very large white rabbit sat, nostrils twitching, jaws chomping, observing her closely. This was his domain. Who was this ridiculous child stretched out before him?

'Hiya, Moby, it's me. Joanne. Did I scare you, old fellow?'

Of the two occupants of the washhouse the rabbit seemed the less agitated. The girl scrambled to her feet with as much dignity as she could muster. Rabbit pellets clung to her trousers. She inspected her knees. Some sort of fungus was sprouting from them. Quickly she wiped it off. She would sponge her tracksuit thoroughly before her mum and Steven returned from the health centre.

'Sorry to disturb you, Moby. I'm just in to have a look at James's old bike. Doing my cycling proficiency at school, you know. Need a set of wheels.'

Joanne was aware that she was babbling on. Rabbiting on! She smiled at the way Old Granny Stewart spoke to each of her six mangy moggies, as if they understood every word she said. Now here she was informing a rabbit as to the purpose behind her visit. Did she need to request the rabbit's permission to enter her own washhouse?

Pulling herself up to her full height of five feet (a slight exaggeration) Joanne peered down at Moby. What a stupid name for a start! A whale's name. Joanne had watched the film one Sunday afternoon. It was boring. A phony-looking whale and a sailor with one leg. Not Long John Silver, another one.

Her dad had chosen the name. Her real dad, not

Ian. He had bought the rabbit from some man in his work for James's birthday. His eighth? Her mum had said it was cruel, keeping a lovely animal penned in a dirty old washhouse. Her mother never came down to see Moby.

According to James, he was a giant New Zealand White. James had researched it in some library book, he said. Joanne could not recall seeing her brother glance at anything other than football magazines.

Joanne bent down and cautiously lifted the rabbit. She could feel his heart trembling beneath the soft white fur. He made no attempt to resist.

'It's alright, boy,' she crooned, stroking an ear gently, 'I'll only be a minute. In you go.' She flipped the latch on the hutch door. Moby gazed out from behind the wire mesh. Joanne couldn't bear to look into those pink eyes.

More light was needed. She pushed the washhouse door open. Motes of dust danced in the beams of sunlight. A spider scuttled across her feet, seeking the comforting shelter of a dark corner. Other unidentifiable bugs seemed content to bask in the warmth of the April sun.

Now that she was able to make a proper examination Joanne decided the washhouse was in some state. Years of neglect had taken their toll of the building. In one corner lay a heap of loose rubble. The rear wall bulged alarmingly. The ceiling looked as if it might cave in at any second. She would not waste time.

Piled against the wall to her right was an assortment of junk: a rusty old cooker, an old-fashioned wringer, various bits of metal which must have formed part of something at one time. There was even the carcass of a pram. Somebody's bogey for the steamie by the look of the odd wheels. Why hadn't her mother tried this establishment for the baby prince's luxury perambulator?

The only object in good condition was Moby's hutch. It had recently been painted, Joanne noticed. James had kept very quiet about this venture. Where had he got the paint and the brushes? On top of the hutch, in neat blue letters contrasting with the white of the roof, he had painted his pet's name 'MOBY DICK McCALLUM'.

Joanne concentrated on the name. She had a sudden insight which would not permit her to dismiss her 'carefree' brother so easily in the future. Hurriedly she shoved this new awareness to the back of her mind. Get the bike and get out, Joanne.

The bicycle was leaning against a radiator. At first sight the prospect did not fill Joanne's heart with joy. For a start it was a yukky reddish-brown colour. Sara would know the proper name for such an ugly shade.

She knew colours like carmine, umber and cobalt blue. Joanne would call this maroon and hope no one looked too closely.

Mr. Greig would look closely. He would go over it with a fine tooth comb. In the interests of safety, of course. He would take one look at the bent front wheel, at the severed brake cable, at the missing light (can you look at something that's not there?), at the catalogue of flaws and defects which constituted this monstrosity and pronounce it useless. No, 'unsatisfactory' he'd say. It just would not do.

Joanne turned away from the bike. 'No luck, Moby. It's hardly a mountain bike, is it?' The prisoner ignored his jailer.

Joanne released the catch on the hutch. Moby remained crouched at the far end. 'Come on, you. Don't go in the huff,' wheedled Joanne. No response.

There was nothing else for it. Joanne snaked her arm round the angle of the opening. The rabbit evaded her initial attempt at capture, hopping over her outstretched fingers. Joanne squeezed her shoulder into the doorway to provide greater reach.

A sharp pain shot through her finger. The beast had bitten her. Well, nipped her. A surge of anger swept through Joanne. She flailed her arm from side to side, banging it off the walls of the hutch. Under her breath she cursed the entire animal kingdom.

Her knuckles clattered against something metallic. Moby forgotten, she groped to discover the unexpected object. Carefully she drew it out. It was a tin box, a treasure chest. James's secret hoard.

Joanne paused. Should she open it? James would never know. No one even knew she was down here.

The temptation was too strong. What could her brother wish to hide from the rest of the family? She raised the lid.

Inside, on the very top, lay a bundle of pound notes held by an elastic band. So this was where he kept the fruits of his paper round. A cursory glance told her that he had saved almost enough for his team's trip to Italy.

Below the money she found his collection of medals. If his side continued to be as successful as this season he would need a larger box. Under the medals she caught a glimpse of a piece of paper. An envelope. A love letter from Sandra Miller?

Joanne took the envelope from the box. It was addressed to James. She felt a faint stirring of recognition as she examined the writing. Trembling, she withdrew the single sheet of cheap notepaper from the envelope. A swift glance at the address at the right-hand corner confirmed her suspicions.

Callander. There was no need to look at the signature at the foot of the page. It was from her father. Her real dad. Joanne could no longer control herself. Feverishly, she read on . . .

'Dear Jim, ...'

Moby, now deigning to vacate his hutch, sat in the middle of the washhouse watching the young girl crying.

CHAPTER

How far away was Callander? In what direction was it? Would she be able to cycle there? If she ever managed to possess a bike, that is.

The next time she went into town she would go to Menzies' and look through their map-books until she located the place. If she had enough cash she might even purchase the appropriate map.

Since finding her father's letter to James, Joanne's emotions had been in turmoil. She considered creating an opportunity to speak with James somewhere private. Maybe even in the washhouse. But what would she say to him? She wanted to tell him that she understood what he was going through.

What about her mother? She had never avoided answering Joanne's questions concerning her dad. She had never tried to portray him as anything other than a man who had loved his children. No, the reason for his leaving had been problems Joanne was too young to appreciate.

Joanne's memory of that period was sketchy.

Raised voices behind closed doors, her father disappearing for days on end, her mother's anxious face and her sudden displays of temper, her father's sheepish return. Until one day he did not return. . . .

Since Ian arrived on the scene Joanne had asked fewer questions. Reluctant though she had been to admit it at first, he had brought a sparkle back into her mother's eyes. At times like this, when he was away working, her mother missed him. Joanne realised that she missed him too. Ian brought a calming influence to the house.

Happiest days of your life! Who would be a child? Joanne struggled with this thought all the way along Paladin Street. She was late. As usual. Sara would be standing outside the park gate waiting for her. As usual.

When Joanne, by now out of breath, turned into Beechwood Road there was no sign of Sara. It was Tuesday. Sara should have been waiting there with her bike, prepared for the afternoon lesson.

Joanne broke into a sort of trot. I must be later than usual. If she had owned a watch she would have consulted it to find out.

Before she reached the park gate Joanne caught sight of her friend through the railings. She was standing in the middle of the main avenue leading up to the gardens. Someone was with her. A scrawny boy with carroty hair. Although Sara's back was to her Joanne knew something was wrong. The manner in which Sara held herself, her arms tightly pressed against her sides, indicated distress.

From the entrance to the park Joanne called to her friend. Sara turned round, a mixture of anxiety and relief registering on her face. Her slight body visibly relaxed. From behind her glasses her moist eyes signalled a message. Help me.

'Hiya, Sara, sorry I'm late,' Joanne began, realising how monotonous this opening line was becoming. 'What's happening?'

'Who's this? The calvary?' interrupted a high-pitched voice. 'Come to rescue you in the nick of time, eh?'

Inside her expensive purple and pink shell-suit Sara squirmed. Joanne glowered at the pathetic specimen of manhood, or rather boyhood, confronting her. If anything she had a slight height advantage over him. She certainly had an advantage in weight. He looked as if a stiff wind might blow him over.

'I think you mean cavalry, don't you?' replied Joanne, correcting a common error among Glasgow children. She knew. Miss Martin had corrected her. 'Calvary was where Jesus was crucified.'

Sara didn't think this was the right time for her

friend to be displaying her undoubted command of general knowledge. 'They've taken my new bike!'

'Who has?' demanded Joanne.

The answer was immediately provided. Over the brow of the hill hurtled Sara's mountain bike. Perched on it was a thickset boy wearing a pale green tracksuit which coincidentally matched the tonings of the bicycle's frame. Aqua Mint finish. If the Park Keeper or Warden or Ranger, or whatever their new title was, caught him he'd be summarily ejected from the park. Why were they never around when you needed them?

The bike skidded to an unnecessarily noisy halt. Gravel chips from the path flicked Joanne's shins. Barely glancing at her the boy dismounted.

He stood a good few inches taller than his mate. In addition, there was a sense of muscularity about him. His face, however, commanded instant attention. It was covered in angry red spots. Furthermore, he had obviously been unable to resist scratching them. Joanne's gaze was transfixed by this raw visage. He seemed vaguely familiar.

'Your shot, Squeak,' the newcomer said. 'Careful not to damage the merchandise, mind.'

Squeak giggled. 'Sure thing, Monty. I'll treat it as if it were my very own.'

'It soon might be!' Monty laughed.

Joanne had had enough. 'Just hold your horses, you two. What do you think you're playing at?'

'We thought we would just take your pal's bike for a wee spin . . .' said the bigger boy.

'And no bring it back!' completed his tiny accomplice.

Joanne stole a quick look at Sara. The tears were about to start flowing again. That would have no effect on these grinning baboons. Sara led too protected an existence. All the money lavished on her didn't prepare her to deal with jokers like these. Instead, she became fair game, a target.

Joanne placed her hand firmly on the saddle of the bike. Dredging up her toughest stare she looked Monty up and down. 'The bike stays with us.'

Monty burst out laughing. He had to admit this tubby little girl had nerve.

Suddenly it clicked with Joanne. She had seen him before. David Montgomery. He had played in the same team as James in Primary. He was in the photograph with the silver trophy.

'I know you!' she exclaimed triumphantly. 'You used to play football with my big brother James.'

'James? James McCallum? Are you James's daft wee sister?' Monty said, all the time maintaining a smile of amusement.

'Aye, and you'd better watch out,' she replied,

warming to her task, 'or I'll get him to give you a right doin'.'

'I'm quaking in my shoes. I admire a girl who's so ready to put her brother's life in danger,' he continued. The grin never left his sore-looking face. 'But for old times' sake Little Lady Muck here can have her precious bike back.'

Squeak started to protest at this unique display of generosity on his friend's part. 'Hey, wait a minute . . .'

'Shut up, Squeak. There are plenty more fish in the sea.'

The ginger-headed dwarf looked puzzled.

'What I mean is,' explained Monty, 'there is a fleet of bikes waiting for us in Helensburgh this weekend. Besides, as my dad used to say, a dog never dirties its own kennel.'

Squeak was none the wiser. He didn't let on. Monty always knew what was best.

Sara clutched her bike before they changed their minds. The boys turned towards the exit. Monty stopped at the bench nearest the gate.

'By the way, if you know anyone interested in purchasing a bike, Monty's Recycled Cycles will be open for business next Tuesday, same time, same place. Racers only £40; Mountain bikes a bargain at £50.'

A dangerous idea flashed through Joanne's head.

'Shoplifters' was Northwood's most thriving commercial concern. Anything from jackets to jacuzzis, carpets to computers, was there if you had the inclination. And the cash.

Joanne knew where to find the cash.

'One last thing,' Monty shouted at her, 'if by chance we should bump into Jimbo this afternoon I'll be delighted to pass on your message.'

As she watched Monty's broad back disappearing through the gate Joanne worried about what she had let her brother in for. Another worry to add to her list. Strolling beside Sara to school she realised how complicated her life had become in the space of one hour. Decisions, decisions, decisions.

CHAPTER

Money burns a hole in your pocket. Another of Nana's favourite sayings. Joanne felt as if her whole body, not just her pocket, was on fire. This must be what guilt feels like.

The money, James's money, was safe in her right-hand pocket, still bound by an elastic band. Her letter to her dad was with it. The key to the washhouse sat in her other pocket. Nobody would miss it till teatime and she'd be back before then.

What was she doing sitting perishing on a park bench when she could be sitting in Miss Martin's warm classroom doing her environmental project? She enjoyed finding out about whales. Their sheer size fascinated her. Kindred spirits, she supposed.

Sara would have to complete their 'Save the Whale' poster by herself. Her friend would wonder what had happened to her. Joanne had fobbed her off with an excuse. Her mum needed her to go to the shops at lunchtime. No, she'd manage fine on her own, thanks. She would meet her in the playground at belltime. Another little lie. The little lies were beginning to mount up.

Joanne knew Sara would disapprove.

The two friends had always confided in one another. Shared secrets. Aired grievances. Hatched plots to outwit sarcastic brothers and suffocating mothers. Many an evening they had huddled together in Sara's bedroom recounting their dreams for the future. Individually each girl lacked confidence; together they could take on the world.

But Sara would not understand this desire, Joanne tried to convince herself. Her friend received everything she wanted; shell-suit, stereo, mountain bike, especially the mountain bike. Deep within Joanne realised she was being unfair to her pal. No amount of money lavished on her could compensate for the misery Sara had experienced.

Back to the business in hand Joanne urged. Where were they? Maybe they didn't come to the park every lunchtime. Would she have to wait until next Tuesday? She needed more information. Just a private chat. No deal. No commitment. Not yet, anyway.

The cold wind brought rain. Joanne had already walked round the small park twice, avoiding the inquisitive stares of the 'parky'. She had visited the gardens, had a shot on the swings, and counted the ducklings in the pond. She had a choice. She could either shelter in the log hut reading the graffiti, love hearts and gang slogans, or catch a bus into the town and see the sights.

Fumbling in her pocket for change she headed for the bus stop.

Joanne got off behind the Savoy Centre. Sauchiehall Street would make a nice change. She wondered if there was a bike shop nearby. Could she stop a stranger to ask without arousing suspicion? Weren't you a bit young to be in town on your own? Shouldn't you be at school? Her mind raced, trying to find plausible answers to these as yet unasked questions.

'Dogging it' was a new experience for Joanne. Plenty of others in her class truanted. Robert Wilson claimed to have run off to London once. But then, he also insisted his father had once nearly been signed by the Rangers. James, she knew, would never 'dog' school. He might miss P.E.

She remembered the money. What if someone suspected she were carrying a large sum of cash. Would a mugger recognise the outline of the bundle of notes? Suddenly the Town didn't seem such a good idea.

She would just go over to Menzies' to check out the map-books and then skedaddle, as Nana would say, back to the security of Northwood. The whole venture had been a mistake. She wasn't cut out to be a thief. If she had been really serious she would have planned things better. How did she think she could explain a mountain bike, even a second-hand one, magically appearing? More importantly, how could the coincidental disappearance of James's Italy money be explained? Most important of all, how could she live with herself if she committed such a despicable act?

A sense of relief swept over Joanne, like a huge weight being lifted from her. She could easily return her brother's hoard and no one need be the wiser. Her sole remaining problem would be a note for Miss Martin. Once she explained everything to her, and apologised for not consulting her in the first place, Sara would forge a splendid note. Diarrhoea, if they could spell it. It was not the sort of complaint her teacher would mention in public.

There was a spring in Joanne's step as she entered the store. Life was (comparatively) good again. Until she spotted them.

Monty and Squeak were hovering near the sweet racks. To a casual observer there was nothing suspicious in two boys choosing a bar of chocolate. Joanne, however, was familiar with the habits of this particular pair.

The skinny red-head selected a slab of fudge and turned to cross to the check-out to pay. As he passed his friend he momentarily shielded Monty from sight. In that fleeting instant, Joanne knew, the bigger boy expertly filched one item, or maybe several, from the shelf. Whatever it was was now concealed within his baggy red and grey shell-suit. In spite of herself she admired his slickness.

Nonchalantly, Monty moved to rejoin his companion. Maintaining a carefree expression he surveyed the store. His eyes met Joanne's. The expression didn't change. There was only the briefest flicker of acknowledgement, imperceptible to a passer-by. Joanne darted up the stairs to the Book Department.

She tried to immerse herself in her search to locate Callander. Joanne was amazed at the ease with which she could switch from one concern to another. For the time being she devoted her concentration to pinpointing the exact spot where her father now lived. It wasn't as far away as she had feared, just beyond Aberfoyle. Ian had driven the family to the David Marshall Lodge in the hills overlooking Aberfoyle last summer. Joanne wondered whether her mum had known how close they were to their dad.

She placed the atlas back on the shelf. Somehow it was reassuring just to have fixed Callander in her head. It was more real to her now.

Monty and Squeak were lounging on the seat

facing the entrance to the shop. Joanne had expected them to get off their marks as soon as they left Menzies'. It was obvious that they were waiting on her.

'Well what do we have here, Squeak,' grinned Monty, 'a new member of the School Un-Appreciation Society?'

Squeak shrieked in his irritatingly piercing fashion.

'Would you care to join us for afternoon tea, young miss?' continued Monty. Not for the first time Joanne wondered why someone so clearly intelligent wasted his days hanging about the streets. 'Here, have a piece of chocolate.'

'No thank you,' Joanne replied, remembering her manners even in this ridiculous situation. At another time she would have killed for a bit of chocolate. 'Anyway, I was under the impression you two were big-time criminals. Knocking sweeties is kids' stuff.'

'Oh this is just . . .' he smirked, tossing a bag to his mate, 'peanuts!' Both boys erupted with laughter. 'Ready salted or honey roast?'

'She looks as if she could scoff both bags,' Squeak chirped. Joanne drew him daggers.

'And why, might I ask, are you not in class?' Monty inquired in his mock-polite style. 'Even my feeble little chum here attended school. A Thursday morning, wasn't it, Squeak?' More laughter.

Joanne hesitated. 'I'm supposed to meet my mum to pick clothes for our holiday. We're going to . . . Callander. For a fortnight.' She hoped no one was keeping tally of these deviations from the truth. Change the subject, Joanne. 'Didn't you say you were going to Helensburgh. Funny place for a holiday!'

'Oh, that's not a holiday, that's a business trip. Confectionery is merely one of several lines we carry.' The big one nudged the little one to supply the punchline.

'Carry away, that is,' added his fellow comedian.

'Or in this case, pedal away,' Monty continued, scratching his acned complexion with a ragged fingernail. 'Supply and demand. At the moment the expanding market is mountain bikes. Last year it was computer games. Before that, skateboards.' He sounded like one of those guys on the whatchamacallit, the Stock Exchange. 'Perhaps madam would care to place an order?'

Joanne felt her face flush. Could he read her mind, like those clairvoyants you read about in the Daily Record who're called in by the police to solve murder mysteries? Or was it a lucky guess? Without thinking her hand moved to her right-hand pocket. She patted the pocket gently. The gesture was not lost on Monty.

Like an angler he let out the line, tempting the fish with the lure.

'Marvellous machines, these mountain bikes. Go anywhere on them; city streets, country roads, and mountains, of course. Reliable too. Not like those skimpy racing bikes. Spend more time mending punctures than cycling.'

Joanne's rapt attention told him she was rising to the bait. Easy does it, now. Soon he would reel her in.

'That's a smasher your pal has. Must have cost a bob or two. Her folk must be loaded, eh? If I was after a set of wheels for myself I'd go for one like that,' Monty sighed.

'But I thought you could supply bikes on request. A minute ago you were taking orders . . .' Joanne's eagerness was tangible. 'Only £50, you said yesterday.'

The 'only' clinched it for Monty. Time to land the catch.

'Oh I can. I have done,' he assured her. 'Half the kids in Paladin Street are riding bikes courtesy of my enterprise. What I meant was that I tend to ply much of my trade in chain stores and in these circumstances a bicycle does not prove much of an asset.'

'Aye, and if Sergeant Aitken caught you on one, Monty, he'd be up at your door with a search warrant to see what else you'd nicked,' piped Squeak.

If looks could kill Squeak would have been in Lambhill cemetery. The mere mention of the police was sufficient to frighten off this particular fish, Monty realised. He could always rely on his dim little friend to sabotage a perfectly brilliant scheme. He shrugged.

Joanne's desire, so overwhelming seconds ago, had all but evaporated. Her previous resolve returned. She would yield not to temptation. She dispelled the nagging doubt that her determination owed more to her fear of being arrested than to her sense of right and wrong.

'I've got to be going,' she said, flustering. 'My mum will wonder where I've got to.'

Neither boy made any attempt to impede her. They knew where she lived. They could always try again. She had just joined their list of prospective customers.

Joanne wandered into Marks and Spencers, weaved her way across the store, and positioned herself on the stairs at the rear. No one was stalking her. She left by the Cambridge Street exit and dashed along to the Savoy Centre. Here she spent twenty minutes losing herself amongst the passageways and stalls. You'd need bloodhounds to trail me, she complimented herself. It was safe to catch a bus home.

Extracting the key from her pocket she unlocked the door to the washhouse. The money would soon be back in its rightful place.

From the first floor landing window of the next close a pair of eyes watched.

CHAPTER

'Where did you get to this afternoon?'

As soon as they were safe within the sanctuary of her bedroom Sara began the interrogation.

Joanne had assumed her customary posture, sprawled on the bed. She attempted to appear relaxed. Sara wasn't fooled. From the superior position of the computer chair she stared down at her uncomfortable friend.

Joanne felt intimidated. She recalled a similar sensation, in Primary Five, when Mrs. Clarke had given her into trouble. The teacher had stood directly in front of Joanne's desk jabbing a bony finger at her. The rings on her hand had glinted in the sunlight. Joanne couldn't remember what her crime had been. In Mrs. Clarke's class she seemed to get into bother regularly. But then, didn't everyone?

'Well, where did you get to?' Sara repeated. 'Needless to say Miss Martin quizzed me. I told her you had complained of pains in your stomach at lunchtime.'

'Thanks, Sara, you're a pal,' Joanne said.

'Don't try to get round me by coming over all sweetness and light. You've got a lot of explaining to do.' Sara was not to be deterred. She had taken a leaf out of her friend's book; Joanne wasn't the only one who could be tough when the occasion demanded.

The bigger girl squirmed, gathered herself, and plunged into her tale. She recounted her escapades of the afternoon. Honesty was the best policy, she decided. She left nothing out. James's money. Waiting in the park. Going into town. Meeting Monty and Squeak. The Temptation. And finally, Doing the Right Thing.

Throughout her account Joanne avoided looking at her friend. She had come to confess. Sara was her conscience, Jiminy Cricket to her Pinocchio.

'Joanne, how could you be so stupid? Dogging school, stealing your own brother's savings, making deals with those . . . those thugs!' Strong words from the polite Sara!

'Honest, Sara, I don't think I would ever have gone through with it. I just kind of borrowed James's money for a wee while,' Joanne offered in self-defence. 'It was nice to dream about buying the bike. Like that time Miss Martin asked what we would do if someone died and left us £100 in their will.'

'And Angela McInnes stood up and said she would

donate it all to charity. "To help the poor little children, Miss." ' Sara mimicked her classmate's syrupy tone.

'What a sook!' Joanne affirmed. 'She wouldn't give you a Smartie if she had a lorry full of them.'

Both girls laughed at their generous classmate.

'What can we do with you?' sighed Sara. Her earlier exasperation had disappeared, to be replaced by bemusement at her friend's antics.

'Well, for a start . . .' Joanne wavered, 'could you maybe write me a note for tomorrow?'

'You are the limit, Joanne McCallum, do you know that? I'm supposed to be your best friend, your only friend, come to think of it, and how do you treat me? You keep things from me. I have to lie for you. I've got to sit here and listen to the scrapes you get yourself into. And now you want me to forge your absence note!'

'It's because you're my best friend that I'm asking you. What are friends for?' Joanne grinned from ear to ear. She recognised Sara's complaint as a token protest. She just needed coaxing.

Sara knew she would abet her friend. Together they would create a wonderful letter capturing the appropriate tone. Inwardly she relished the notion of being an accomplice in Joanne's misdemeanour. Her mother would definitely not approve.

'Before we get down to writing the note, Sara, there's something else I want to show you.' From her bag Joanne brought out the letter she had written to her father. 'Would you read this for me, please. I'm not sure I'm doing the right thing. . . .'

Carefully Sara skimmed through the letter. When she had finished she took off her glasses and rubbed her eyes. Joanne fiddled with a loose strand of hair, nervously twirling it between her fingers.

'Do you think its okay to send it?' she asked at last.

Sara's mind was working overtime. The letter presented all sorts of problems. What would Mrs. Gordon say if she discovered Joanne was writing to her dad? Did he really want to hear from her after all this time? How could he get in touch with Joanne? Her mum would hardly welcome correspondence from him. One question predominated.

'Do you want to send it? What I mean is, are you sure you want to go through with this? You don't know where it might lead. . . .'

'I know what you're trying to say,' Joanne answered, 'but I want to let him know that I still care. Maybe he thinks I hate him or something. He's still my dad, Sara.'

'What about your mum? And Ian?' her friend felt compelled to ask.

'Och, I love my mum, you know that. Even when

we're not on speaking terms. And I know she's a lot happier now that Ian's on the scene. But I've still got a right to keep in touch with my own father, haven't I?'

Sara didn't look too convinced.

'Don't worry, I'm not going to run away to the wilds of Callander,' Joanne reassured her. 'I like my home comforts too much.'

'Well, if your mind's made up,' Sara conceded, 'post it off.' She was still uncertain as to the soundness of this advice. The whole affair could explode in Joanne's face.

Joanne replaced the letter in her bag. She'd buy a stamp in the morning and send it away. And lie in wait each morning to intercept the postwoman.

'Come on, let's get your note written,' urged Sara, 'and then I will tell you my news.'

Joanne's interest was aroused by her pal's deliberately teasing tone. 'What news? Don't be mean, Sara. Tell me now. Is it about Alison Buchanan and Jimmy McGill?'

'I said news, not gossip,' Sara replied sharply. 'It's something of special interest to you, as a matter of fact. Something you would have found out if you had attended school this afternoon instead of gallivanting round the town.'

Joanne hated it when Sara adopted that lofty, self righteous tone. She hated it even more when she was left in the dark. Something of interest to her? No point in arguing when Sara was in this no-nonsense mood. Write the letter.

Working in harmony the two girls rapidly constructed a satisfactory note accounting for Joanne's absence. It was almost a work of art. Joanne had to persuade Sara to end the letter with 'and Oblige'. Neither girl understood this strange finale. Sara's mum certainly never wrote it. But Joanne insisted that every note she had ever taken to school contained this concluding phrase.

Having deposited the note in her bag alongside the letter to her father Joanne turned to her friend. 'Please, Miss, I've finished my assignment. Can I get my treat now?'

'Oh very well,' Sara said, folding her arms across her chest in a manner reminiscent of their teacher. 'Now close your eyes, little girl, and don't open them until I tell you.'

Joanne complied with this instruction. Sara opened a buff folder lying next to her computer. She withdrew a sheet of paper and placed it on Joanne's lap. Automatically her eyes opened.

'What's this?' she asked.

'You shall go to the ball, Cinderella,' said the apprentice Fairy Godmother. 'Perhaps not in a glass coach, but maybe on a mountain bike.'

Joanne pored over the sheet. It was an entry form for a competition. To win a bike. Her pulse was racing. She experienced a tingling sensation. Did she dare to hope?

'If, as I've stated several times this evening, you had managed to drag yourself into school you would have been given all the requisite information,' pronounced Sara, enjoying the opportunity to show off her familiarity with 'big words'. 'Miss Martin entrusted me to give out these forms, so naturally I snaffled one for you.'

At the top of the sheet was an illustration of one of the latest bicycles. Joanne recognised it as a Mustang. Eagerly she devoured the details of the competition printed beneath. A local shop, her local shop, 'Deals on Wheels', was offering a grand prize of a bicycle 'of your choice' to the winner. All you had to do was write an essay explaining why you wanted to own a bike and how you would spend your first day with your new acquisition. All!

Joanne's spirits, which had been soaring like a bird moments earlier, suddenly plummeted. The competition was open to anyone who cared to enter. What chance did she have? Some swotty wee kid from Castleton would walk off, or rather, ride off with the prize.

Sara continued filling in the details. 'The man in

the shop, your pal Mr. Ross, is circulating all the local schools. Good publicity, I suppose. Plus there's to be an advert in the "Argus", maybe even "The Daily Record". For the doggers. . . .' She couldn't resist this last dig at her friend. 'Just think, Joanne, your picture in the papers. . . .'

'I've no chance,' Joanne moaned. 'There will be millions of folk going in for it.'

'Well, you've certainly got no chance with that attitude,' reproved Sara. 'In any case, Miss Martin is insisting the whole class enters the competition. Look at this.'

Picking up the buff wallet again, she took out a sheaf of papers. An essay, five pages long, perfectly set out and printed, was passed to Joanne.

'My dad let me use his Apple to key in my effort. Then he printed it out for me.'

It was impressive. Joanne's spirits touched rock bottom. How could she hope to compete with the wonders of modern technology? The pen is mightier than the sword Miss Martin had said. But is it mightier than the computer chip?

'You've already got a bike,' protested Joanne, 'and here you are putting in this . . . , this . . . masterpiece! Nobody else will have a look in.'

Sara hadn't considered this view. Trying to do one's best, no matter what the activity, was the only approach she knew. What else was she supposed to do?

Joanne glanced at the clock on Sara's bedside table. 'I'll have to get on my way. My mum is expecting me back by nine.' This was true, but it sounded feeble. 'I'll take the form and give it a shot. What have I got to lose?'

Sara shook her head in silent despair. Whatever had happened to the happy-go-lucky Joanne she used to know? Well, she'd put on the beef for a start, but she was hardly your jolly fat person. She found herself voicing this opinion out loud.

'You're a real misery, do you know that? Time to buck up your ideas. Be positive. You want to write to your dad, so do it. You want a bike, so get cracking on this daft essay.'

Joanne counterfeited a smile. If you come to your friend for advice you have to be prepared to accept it.

Sara accompanied Joanne down the garden path to the gate. There was a tense silence. Up until a few days ago their relationship had been easy-going, almost boring at times. The recent revelations had both deepened and strained their friendship.

Summoning up a cheerful grin Joanne set off home. Sara watched her until she reached the end of Alba Avenue. Joanne stopped to wave before turning the corner.

Upstairs once more, Sara selected a ballpoint pen from her collection. From her large notepad she tore half a dozen sheets of lined paper. She placed the immaculate print-out of her essay on her desk and began laboriously copying it out in long-hand.

CHAPTER

'What is this? And this?'

The voice seemed to be coming through a fog. It was muffled. Joanne felt she should be able to identify it but it kept drifting away just as she thought she recognised it.

She snuggled deeper into her pillow and tried to re-enter the world of sleep. Something always disturbed you just as you reached the really good bit in your dream. She had been cycling through the countryside. Her and Sara. Some place she'd never been. With lots of tall, bushy trees. The sky was so blue. Someone was singing. It was her. . . .

A hand on her shoulder dragged her into consciousness. She could only faintly hear her song. The hand was persistent; it shook her until her eyes blinked open. Through the haze a figure formed. Her mother. She had a white flag in her hand. Was she surrendering?

Joanne attempted to sweep the mist from her sight with the back of her right hand. Objects in the room took on a definite shape. Yes, there was the wardrobe. Jackie must have left the door open as usual. There was the chair. Piled high with Jackie's clothes. They should have been in the wardrobe. Or in the wash.

'I'll ask you again, my girl. What are these?'

Her mum was waving two flags now, one in either hand. Only they weren't flags. They were pieces of paper. Letters. Before Joanne could marshal her explanations, rescue came from an unexpected source.

'Mum, have you seen my shinguards?' James called from the kitchen. 'I need them for the game. F.I.F.A. regulation, mum.'

Margaret Gordon hadn't a clue what these initials represented. Football and its mysteries remained just that, a mystery. Twenty-two men (she at least got the number correct) pursuing an inflated leather sphere around a field in an effort to propel it between some poles stuck at either end of a decent piece of grass seemed the height of absurdity. No, take that back. Grown men becoming agitated watching this spectacle was even more ridiculous. She realised her views were blasphemous in a city where football was to many the one true religion.

'I'm coming, I'm coming,' she shouted. 'You should have looked them out last night.' She fluttered the letters in front of Joanne's face. 'We'll have a discussion about this once your brother has left for school.'

Alone in her room, Joanne sat up in bed and stared straight at the door ahead. A kind of numbness had set in. Her body was rigid, her fists clenched so tightly that the nails dug into her palms. She was unaware. All her justifications for contacting her father had evaporated with the heat of her mother's emotion. Her strength of will had been drained, leaving this husk.

Several minutes passed. Muted voices filtered through from next door. The ugly racket of Paladin Street traffic seeped in the window. Directly below the Dalziels' radio commenced its insistent din. Try as she might Joanne could not prevent reality from intruding. This was no dream.

In a very controlled manner she threw back the duvet, swivelled her legs out of bed and stood up. Methodically she gathered her clothes from the chair and headed for the bathroom, where she snibbed the door behind her.

She followed the normal pattern of her morning preparation. She turned on the shower, adjusting the dial to the warmer temperature she preferred. She placed her towel on the side of the bath. She checked that James had not used up all the liquid soap her mother had taken to purchasing lately.

Finally, as she did each day, she struggled out of

her nightie and stepped onto the bathroom scales. She was two pounds lighter; her secret diet was working. On any other day this would have been cause for celebration. Today it seemed irrelevant.

Stepping into the shower she allowed the warm stream to envelop her. It comforted. The steady tattoo of the jets of water onto the plastic base provided a soothing rhythm. Shortly she would have to face the music.

In the kitchen Margaret Gordon pottered about, seeking to immerse herself in the mundane routine of dispatching her assorted children to school and work.

Jackie had already gone. Late as usual, she had no time to sit down to breakfast. A roll from Malik's, eaten on the bus, would suffice.

The slurping from the direction of the table told her that James had nearly finished his bowl of cereal. A glass of milk to follow the half-pint in which he drowned his corn-flakes and he'd be off. From the tin on top of the fridge he would take a chocolate biscuit for his 'playpiece'. He always pocketed two biscuits. Any discrepancy would be laid at Joanne's door. His mother was well aware of this practice. She just didn't let James know that she was on to his game.

Steven lay peacefully in his cot. The sleep of the innocent. At six o'clock he had roused her, been duly fed and changed, and returned to his cot. Margaret appreciated the tranquility of that hour between her older children's departure and the baby waking again.

'I'm away, mum. We've got a semi against Kelvin this afternoon, so I'll be a bit late.'

Mrs. Gordon kissed her son lightly on the cheek. This morning ritual was the only show of affection he would tolerate. And then, only if they were alone.

'Have a good game,' she said to his retreating figure, 'and I hope you win.'

'Of course we will,' he said confidently. 'Easy! Cup Final next week, no bother.'

Margaret carried James's dishes to the sink. She wished that Joanne shared her brother's effervescent nature. Nothing knocked him off his stride. His aim in life was to have as much fun as possible.

'Enjoy life,' her own mother would say, 'for you'll be a long time dead.'

Joanne, on the other hand, was deep. 'Thinks too much, that one,' pronounced her gran, her Nana. Since when was thinking a crime? Margaret Gordon had high hopes for her younger daughter. She was the one with brains in the family. One who might escape.

A twinge of conscience needled Margaret. She hadn't been searching through Joanne's bag. Well, she had been, but legitimately. For the monthly newssheet from Mrs. Thompson outlining the forthcoming activities. There should be a Parents' Night at the Big

School soon for all those whose kids were coming up after the holidays.

The newssheet wasn't in evidence. But there, as large as life, was this note for Miss Martin and the letter to John.

She had always prided herself that she was the type of parent who trusted her children. Okay, Jackie had been a bit wild at one point, but that was only a phase. No, bring them up properly, show them love and respect, and they would give you it in return. And now this. . . .

Funny, you thought you were doing the right thing. At the time of the break-up she had tried to explain the situation to each of them. She had never openly criticised their father. Indeed, she found herself at times defending him from Jackie's savage attacks.

When she met Ian she had been at pains to introduce him gradually into the house. He wasn't a replacement; he didn't want to be. The kids liked him. They had had some great times together. The whole household missed him when he was away on the rigs.

She knew she shouldn't have opened Joanne's letter. That was the sort of sneaky thing her mother would do. Margaret Livingstone had promised herself that if she ever had children she would treat them fairly. She had suffered from her mother's nosiness, her need to know all your business.

She had resisted at first. Open the note to the teacher, a tiny voice had whispered. You're entitled to know what's in that, surely. She didn't take much convincing.

She was genuinely shocked by the revelation that Joanne had stayed away from school yesterday afternoon. Oh, there was an epidemic of truancy in the area, she knew. You couldn't walk down Paladin Street on a sunny day without tripping over kids 'dogging' it. Kids just walking about aimlessly. But her Joanne?

Margaret had felt stupid. Maybe she had been blind, ignored the signs. Other people's children went walkabout. Not hers. But now . . . For how long? And how often?

The second letter had been torn open in anger. She needed someone to blame. Her daughter went behind her back. She had failed as a mother. Why not take her wrath out on John? He was well out of it, wasn't he?

The contents of the letter had been little more than a blur. Writing it was enough. She had rampaged through to the bedroom, ready to do battle. With an eleven-year-old girl . . . With her big, cuddly daughter . . . Her other baby.

The twinge had become an ache. Margaret had

handled the whole matter wrongly. Totally wrongly. Sure, I can sit down and talk to my kids. We have a good relationship. Sure.

Margaret knew what she had to do. Apologise to Joanne. Find time to talk things over. Get to the root of the problem. She would write a note to Miss Martin covering yesterday. She would post the letter to Callander. Perhaps include a few words herself. . . .

She set a bowl for Joanne on the table. She collected herself, aware that she was trembling. Slowly, she walked through to the girls' room, practising her lines.

The room was empty. The house seemed suddenly empty.

CHAPTER

In normal circumstances you would have witnessed Joanne rushing home after school. Teatime television exerted a vice-like grip on the young population. But today had not been normal.

Joanne found herself delaying her return to 472 Paladin Street for as long a period as she could without incurring more trouble. Her steps dragged as she allowed each shop window she passed to distract her. Paladin Street contained a fair number of shops.

By night these shops wore a suit of armour. Mesh, grilles and shutters formed a visor from behind which the goods glared defiantly. Just now they showed their welcoming face, greeting passers-by as old friends, inviting them to enter and browse.

Her mother frequently complained about the lack of choice offered. This didn't bother Joanne. So what if there were five different bakeries? Such an abundance permitted her to press her nose against each in turn while she decided which confectionery delight she would choose. Supposing she had any money. Supposing she abandoned her diet.

The four hairdressing salons didn't interest her in quite the same way. Nor did the three shoe shops. 'Top and toe,' her mum had said witheringly, 'top and toe. They think if they provide women with fancy footwear and fancier hair-dos that will keep us quiet.' Joanne wasn't sure who 'they' were.

There were various clothes shops on either side of the street. On occasion her mother had bought the odd tee-shirt or pair of socks for Joanne or James, nothing very stylish. Joanne much preferred accompanying Jackie to her work and selecting something fashionable from the row upon row of fabulous stuff on display. For all her faults Jackie could be quite generous when the mood took her.

Only the cycle shop drew Joanne like a magnet towards it. Regularly, without intending, she was irresistibly attracted to its doorway. Standing on the threshold she would gaze awestruck at the twin rows of bikes suspended from the ceiling. Each wheel with its gleaming spokes was a magic disc, ready to whisk her off to unknown lands.

'Penny for them,' said the wiry figure emerging from behind an upturned bicycle. A broad grin seemed to take up most of his nut-brown face.

Automatically, Joanne smiled back. The good

humour of this wee man was infectious. 'Oh I wasn't really thinking about anything,' she replied, 'just looking, as usual.'

Jockey Ross beckoned her into the shop. She gladly followed him between the aisles of shiny machines to the counter at the rear of his shop. He had a slightly bandy-legged gait which Joanne attributed to his years of cycling.

When he first opened 'Deals on Wheels' some months back he cut quite a figure in Paladin Street. His customary attire in the shop was full racing gear: gaudy, multi-coloured vests covered in advertising logos, tight cycling shorts, and those funny shoes, like ballet pumps, racers wore. Today he was wearing a yellow and blue top with some foreign name slashed across the chest. Joanne thought it was French, but it could have been Italian.

Ian had told her that, in his day, Jockey Ross had been one of Scotland's best road racers. Eddie Ross, known to all cycling enthusiasts as Jockey because of his skill in manoeuvring himself into the right position from which to attack, had carried the flag for his country against the finest opposition from Eastern Europe.

Walking behind him, Joanne felt large and clumsy. This compact little man could just as easily have passed for a jockey in the Grand National.

'Have you picked up one of these?' he asked, handing her a competition entry.

The sound of a fire engine siren, like an asthmatic dinosaur, drowned out her reply. She nodded instead. When she was younger she and the other children in the street had trailed fire engines and ambulances with the prospect of some excitement. Today, bicycles offered more chance of adventure.

'They gave us one at school,' she said when the noise had faded. 'Everybody I know is entering.'

Jockey Ross detected a note of depression in the girl's voice. When Frank, his partner, had suggested the competition they had hoped it would stimulate local interest in the shop and in cycling in general. It was discouraging to see this young girl so pessimistic. It was supposed to be a harmless piece of fun.

He still had a great deal to learn about business, he thought. When the engineering works had closed down and he and Frank had been made redundant the idea of opening a cycle shop seemed very attractive. They had their redundancy money to start them off. Jockey had provided enough running capital by selling his house in Scotstoun. With Ellen gone what did he need a big house with a garden for anyway?

He remembered Ellen bent over hoeing as he wheeled his bike up the path. She never asked the result. She wouldn't even glance up from the border.

'Get the kettle on for a cup of tea,' she would command, 'and then you can tell me all about your wee run in the country.'

Jockey missed her. He had rattled about in that house for the best part of a year. Selling up and moving back to Partick was the logical idea. Irene wanted him to live with her in Toronto, but when you've been a person in your own right who wants to be known as someone's father or grandfather?

'If you win what will you choose?' he asked, sustaining his grin. 'A mountain bike like your wee pal, I'll bet.'

He had tried to persuade Mr. Devlin that an ordinary bike was sufficient for city cycling, but Sara had her heart set on a mountain bike. 'Fashion dictates business' Frank often stated. 'The customer is always right' was his other slogan.

'Fat chance I have of winning,' Joanne muttered.

Immediately she covered her mouth with her hand to prevent herself laughing at her accidental joke. Jockey wasn't so courteous. A raucous roar shook his sinewy frame.

'I've an even slimmer chance,' he said, hardly able to speak for laughing, 'and do you know why?'

'No,' Joanne answered.

'Because I'm skint. You could say I'm having a lean time of it,' he guffawed.

'Well I've got a few extra pounds I could lend you,' Joanne continued, enjoying this banter with the wee cyclist.

Both participants called a halt to the joke session. It had served to cheer each of them. They exchanged broad smiles. Joanne felt slightly embarrassed. She wasn't used to being so relaxed with a relative stranger. Jockey Ross had that effect on people.

'You'll have to come here everyday,' he said. 'We could form a double act. "Jockey and . . ." '

'. . . the Horse,' Joanne giggled.

'Now be serious for a minute. I don't even know your name and you must be goggling in that window every second day.'

'It's Joanne,' she said, 'Joanne McCal . . . Joanne Gordon.'

'Well, Joanne Gordon, I'll look forward to reading your story. Be sure to put a joke or two in it. I like a good laugh.'

Joanne assured him that she would. Still grinning from ear to ear he escorted her to the door.

'See you soon, I'm sure,' Jockey said as she stepped out into Paladin Street.

'Bye, Mr. Ross,' Joanne said.

'Jockey. I'm Jockey to my friends, Joanne,' the little man smiled. 'Don't forget to get a few laughs in.'

'I won't,' Joanne replied and danced off home.

CHAPTER

Her close. They were outside her close. A big red fire engine and an ambulance. And a huge crowd of people.

Strangely there was no evidence of any fire. No smoke billowed from the building. The acrid smell of burning material was absent. That peculiar crackling noise as flames devoured wood was not to be heard.

The proximity of the spectators confirmed that there was little danger. Joanne identified distinct groups of by-standers. Gathered near the ambulance was the Coven, her mother's term for the middle-aged women who constituted the local gossip column. Standing half on the pavement, half on the road, was the Quality Street Gang who had abandoned their post at the Cross, bringing their refreshment with them. Squads of kids milled about, forming and dissolving temporary alliances in an amoeba-like fashion.

Snippets of conversations wafted towards Joanne as she approached the scene.

'There's a dead body in there . . .'

'Blood all over the place, I heard . . .'

'Head squashed like a tomato . . .'

Children take a gruesome delight in gory details. The popularity of 'slash and maim' video 'nasties' is ample testimony to this. Joanne recognised some of her classmates among these ghouls.

Her pulse raced as she pushed her way through the mob. A body? Fear ran its icy fingertips down her spine.

'I blame the District Council. Those washhouses should have been pulled down years ago,' Mrs. Shearer volunteered to her bingo buddy, Mrs. Dunbar.

'I quite agree, Sadie,' returned her crony, 'I've always said there would be an accident one of these days.'

'Shouldn't be keeping pets in them in any case,' chipped in the third of the witches, Mrs. McCluskey. 'Encourages vermin.'

'Should be no pets in closes either,' Mrs. Shearer pronounced. 'That bunch of dirty toerags below me have got one of those "devil dogs" . . .'

'Rottweilers,' informed Mrs. Dunbar.

'Exactly, Agnes,' continued Mrs. Shearer, 'and I'm terrified to go up and down my own stair.'

Icy fingertips clenched into a fist. Joanne used her bulk to force a path to the front of the crowd. James!

She had seen for herself how unsafe that wall had been.

'It's Maggie Livingstone's wean,' Mrs. McCluskey said, 'wee Joanne.'

'Don't you worry yourself, hen,' Mrs. Dunbar consoled, 'he's maybe not that hurt.'

The icy fist squeezed tighter. Job's Comforter, her Nana would call this interfering old biddy.

'Let me past!' screamed Joanne. 'It's my brother in there!'

The Quality Street Gang surfaced from their alcoholic haze to register this newcomer. Dolly Davie almost released his hold on his can of 'super' lager, surprised at this sudden outburst. A look of stupefied sympathy appeared on Betty the Bag's swollen red features.

The firm hand of Sergeant Aitken halted Joanne's progress.

'No one is allowed through,' the giant policeman grunted. 'Just let them get on with their job.'

Black jackets and yellow helmets could be glimpsed at the far end of the close. Some seemed to be dragging rubble aside. The whole front of the washhouse had collapsed. A cloud of dust and grime obscured her vision.

Joanne could take no more. She barged past the policeman, dunting him with her shoulder in the process. One or two children cheered at the sight of their arch-enemy colliding with the wall of the close. The hefty sergeant had no time to consider this affront to his dignity. He set off in pursuit.

Joanne reached the back court. It looked as if a bomb had struck the washhouse. Not only the front wall, but also half the roof had caved in. The firemen were attempting to clear debris to allow them access to the trapped boy.

The Fire Officer directing operations grabbed her as she dashed towards the washhouse. He held her fast despite her wriggling and squirming.

'Parker, take this tiger off my hands,' he yelled at a fireman, busy hauling bricks to one side. 'Get her out of the way.'

Sergeant Aitken, relieved to see someone else given this task, sloped off.

Fireman Parker glowered at Joanne. Looking after children was not a duty of the Fire Brigade.

'Over here, you,' Parker said, towing Joanne to the far corner of the back court. Joanne felt unnecessary force was used.

As soon as Parker spoke Joanne realised that this fireman was a firewoman! Or should that be a fireperson? She hadn't known that such creatures existed.

Alison Parker didn't take too kindly to babysitting

a young girl. Why couldn't one of the guys do it? She had not struggled to be accepted in the service only to be fobbed off with what unliberated men saw as women's work! Let Joe or Alec pat this kid on the head and shut her up with a lollipop.

'Is he okay?' Joanne pleaded. The concern in her voice softened Alison's initial annoyance. 'Please say he's alright.'

'His legs are trapped, probably broken. But it doesn't look as if he's damaged anything else.'

His legs! James would be distraught. All his plans. Cup ties. League titles. Football in Italy this summer. Now he'd stay at home while his team-mates flew off to Milan.

'What was he doing in there anyway?' asked the fireperson.

'Feeding his pet rabbit, Moby,' Joanne answered.

'Oh. No sign of any rabbit, I'm afraid. I'm sorry.' Parker sounded genuinely upset.

A sudden commotion from the close distracted everyone. Sergeant Aitken's deep rumble could be heard remonstrating with someone.

'Joanne! Joanne! Come out here.' It was her mum.

Joanne rushed to the close, Parker in attendance. There stood her mother with an abashed Sergeant Aitken. Steven was propped up in his new pram, bright-eyed as usual. And behind them, a carrier bag of messages in either hand, was James.

James! Without hesitating Joanne rushed forward and embraced her brother. She hugged and hugged him, pinning his arms to his sides. The assembled multitude in Paladin Street roared their approval.

James's face turned scarlet. You score two goals to take the club through to the final. You should expect a hero's welcome. Instead your mum collars you in the street and makes you carry the shopping home. In front of the whole team! Now your fat wee sister gives you big sloppy kisses with the entire population of Northwood watching! How would he ever live this down?

'Gangway! Make room for the stretcher,' cried the ambulancemen. The Gordons joined the rest of Paladin Street on the pavement. James took the opportunity to set down his bags and go over to stand with his grinning mates.

Curiosity dominated Joanne. If it wasn't James, then who was it?

Her question was soon answered. The stretcher re-emerged, blanket drawn up to the chin of the patient. Above the blanket was a shock of red hair, sprinkled with a light coating of dust.

Squeak!

As they lifted him into the ambulance, Joanne saw

Monty hovering on the fringe of the crowd. His face was ashen. He caught Joanne's gaze, shrugged and turned away.

'We found this,' Alison Parker said, handing Joanne a battered tin box.

James's money box. The pieces of the jigsaw began to fit into place. Quickly Joanne checked the contents. Nothing had been removed. She breathed a sigh of relief.

Two streets away a large white rabbit was tucking into some unsuspecting gardener's prize lettuce.

CHAPTER

The official version of the day's events, the one related to Jackie on her return from the shop, was that young Tony McGowan, to give Squeak his proper title, had heard a noise coming from the washhouse, presumably from the unfortunate Moby, had tried to investigate and in pursuit of this investigation had succeeded in bringing the washhouse down on top of himself.

The 'official version' was determined and disseminated by the Bingo Buddies.

No one believed the official version.

Sergeant Aitken had encountered Master McGowan too often in suspicious circumstances to countenance his attempted rescue of a poor little furry animal.

James considered the proximity of Squeak to his secret treasure chest to be too much of a coincidence.

Margaret Gordon wasn't quite sure what was going on but she knew from Joanne's behaviour that there was more to this episode than met the eye.

Joanne was experiencing a peculiar mixture of relief and trepidation. James was safe, the money box had been recovered, and no one was aware of her role in leading Squeak, unwittingly, certainly, to the hiding place. But for how long? What if Squeak blurted out the whole sorry story? She'd watched a film once where the hero had been given some drug which made him tell all the secret plans. What if Squeak, under anaesthetic, mentioned her encounters with him and Monty?

She thrust this worry to the back of her mind. She knew it was a case of her guilty conscience tormenting her. She'd had a real fright. She'd learned her lesson. From now on she would keep on the straight and narrow, as Nana called it.

The washhouse incident had dominated tea-time conversation. It made a welcome change from Jackie's blow by blow account of the thrills of being a shop assistant. Even James was prepared to forego the match commentary on his team's latest and greatest victory. And no reference was made to the two letters brandished about this morning. Somehow her mother's silence only served to increase Joanne's concern.

Margaret Gordon drained the last drop of tea from her china cup. The cup and saucer had taken her fancy when Ian had taken them through to West Kilbride for the day last summer. She knew it was impractical to use fine china. Joanne was never permitted to wash it. But Margaret appreciated its delicacy and the elegant hand-painted pattern on the side of the cup. Although she knew it was an indulgence she had not protested when Ian had insisted on buying it for her.

Their mother's setting down of her prize possession acted as the signal for the children to leave the table. Three chairs were pushed back, three bodies rose to go about their business.

'Just hold on a minute,' Mrs. Gordon commanded. 'I know it's been an exciting day for each of you and the tension has exhausted you, but there are a few things about the house to be dealt with before you disappear into your bedrooms.'

Three faces scowled at her. Three mouths opened ready to contend this statement.

Jackie, by far the most garrulous of the brood, got in first. 'But, mum, Sean's supposed to be meeting me in an hour. We're going into town to. . . .'

Margaret raised her hand, palm open, signalling the end of Jackie's protestations. 'Not another word. I don't wish to hear his name until you've managed to clear away all the clothes which are presently cluttering up your room. I do your washing for you. I do virtually all your ironing, except the things you always seem to need at the last minute. At least you could bother to hang your clothes up. Remember,

Joanne has to share that room. Why should she live in a coup?'

Jackie grimaced at Joanne as if she had been the cause of her mother issuing this decree. Joanne looked bemused. Inwardly she was delighted that her messy sister was finally being taken to task. She had complained often and loudly about the state of their bedroom. Why today of all days was her mum displaying this regard for her wellbeing?

With as bad grace as she could muster, Jackie left the kitchen. Mrs. Gordon couldn't resist one final dig at her huffy daughter. 'I hope Sean knows what cookers, hoovers, and washing machines are for, miss, or the pair of you will be in a sorry state.'

A door banged.

During this altercation James had been attempting to slip unnoticed from the kitchen. He had negotiated the table, sundry chairs, Joanne, and was now stationed clutching the door handle.

'Where are you slinking off to?' Margaret's gaze pinned her son to the wall. 'Has the Rangers' manager called you into his squad?'

'No,' replied James, feeling foolish at his instinctive response to his mother's sarcastic suggestion. 'Eh . . . I thought I might go out and search for Moby.'

Joanne had to give her brother credit for quick thinking.

'That's a good idea,' Mrs. Gordon admitted, 'but it can wait until after you've emptied your football bag and put your smelly socks and shorts in the wash-basket.'

James knew better than to argue with his mum when she was in one of her authoritative moods. She would only find other wee jobs for him to do.

'And you can take your sister with you on this mission of mercy. She can act as the guide to make sure the expedition doesn't end up at the football pitch.'

Both her remaining offspring stared at her in disbelief. James and Joanne didn't even acknowledge one another if they passed in the street. The thought of spending an evening together hunting round Northwood. . . .

'Oh don't look so shocked. The two of you were quite lovey-dovey this afternoon,' joked Margaret. 'It was very touching.'

James and Joanne blushed at the memory and edged further apart.

'Right, Joanne, I'll wash and you can dry,' she continued, tossing a tea-towel in Joanne's general direction. Joanne retrieved it from the floor. James made his escape before he was asked to put the dishes away.

Margaret Gordon gathered the tea dishes on the worktop beside the sink. She found herself humming a tune, some hit from the seventies. Despite her firmness with the children she was in a cheerful mood. She felt she had handled bringing them into line in a fairly good-humoured fashion. And also, accidents had a way of reminding you how valuable your kids were.

'Before we get started there's a letter for school behind the picture on the mantelpiece. I said that you were suffering from stomach pains after lunch. I only hope my reputation as a cook isn't affected. . . .'

Her mum's light-hearted tone confused Joanne. She had anticipated a full-scale barney, had expected to receive a real tongue-lashing. She recalled the blistering verbal assaults on Jackie. Not that Jackie didn't give as good as she got.

This gentle approach increased Joanne's sense of guilt. Sometimes she underestimated her mother's sensitivity.

'Mum, I'm sorry,' she said, looking directly into her mother's eyes. 'I guess I didn't think about what I was doing. You see, I wanted this bike so much. . . .'

'Don't try to explain just now, Joanne. I know you'll have had your reasons. When we've both had a chance to consider all that's happened we'll sit down and discuss it. Maybe in a day or two.'

Margaret placed her hands on her daughter's shoulders. She squeezed them affectionately. Both mother and daughter were conscious that tears would soon begin to flow.

'As for the other matter, the letter to your father, I posted it for you this afternoon. I think all of us, you, me, your brother and sister, need to have a good heart to heart talk. Maybe I've taken too much for granted. . . .'

It was Joanne's turn to hug her mother. For a full minute they clung to one another, closer than words.

'This isn't getting the dishes done, milady,' commented Margaret eventually, untangling herself. 'Now go and put that note in your bag before you forget it.'

Joanne extracted the envelope from behind the photograph Ian had taken of Margaret and the children at the Garden Festival.

'Mum . . .' she began, emotion welling up inside her.

'Away you go, you big lump, or I'll be washing these plates in salt water.'

CHAPTER

Northwood was not noted for its greenery. Given its title, one might have expected to encounter, if not an impenetrable forest, at least a small grove of staunch old trees surviving from a time before civilisation reached this far-flung part of the kingdom. But there was no forest, no grove, no copse, not even an experimental avenue. There was only the park where elms and birches stood unrecognised behind bars.

The locals had long since given up trying to fathom out why their area was thus named. Glasgow's city fathers, in their wisdom, had bestowed attractive but meaningless names on many districts. If challenged they would dredge up old maps and records proving the antiquity of these tags. But the people were not so easily fooled. Pleasant titles disguised ugly reality. Drumchapel. Easterhouse. Castlemilk. Lovely names all.

James and Joanne headed towards Saint Mungo's Hill. The tussocky strips of grass in front of the tenements afforded no shelter for a creature as visible as Moby. In any case he would have found little sustenance amongst the discarded cans and assorted debris which casually littered the majority of the 'gardens'. Any intelligent rabbit would seek out the greener pastures of the Hill.

On setting out on their quest they had maintained a discreet distance between each other. Two mothers strolling side by side with their prams could (and did) pass comfortably through the gap. As brother and sister progressed, however, they gradually drew closer together. Each was by nature a talker. Silence was difficult to sustain.

Besides, James had questions he wanted to ask. The pieces of the jigsaw were scattered in front of him. Joanne had hidden the lid of the box. How did Squeak know that he concealed his savings in the old washhouse? Why had his not-so-little sister smothered him in hugs and kisses?

'Jo-Jo,' he began, adopting a matter-of-fact tone, 'how long do you think Squeak will be in the hospital?'

Joanne's antenna sensed something amiss in her brother's sudden concern for the scoundrelly redhead. 'A few weeks, maybe. A month?' She tried to sound vaguely disinterested. 'Depends on how bad he is.'

He was very bad, she thought. Extremely wicked.

Perhaps he might never walk again. Have to get around in a wheelchair. Now she was being wicked. A bit of physical discomfort and several weeks of hospital food should teach him a lesson.

'I was just wondering,' James continued, 'whether we should visit him. Take a bunch of grapes, that sort of thing.'

Joanne gulped audibly.

'After all, he was only trying to help. He didn't know Moby was a pet, did he? Probably thought he was freeing a trapped cat or something.'

Freeing your money, Joanne thought. Her skin felt clammy, sticky, wet, now hot, now cool. She struggled to control her breathing, taking long deep breaths. A vice gripped her skull, a cap of metal bands, tightening, crushing her head, squeezing her brain until it exploded. James's voice droned on.

'Wonder what he was doing round our bit? Stays over the bridge, in the Glen, doesn't he?'

'I don't know,' croaked Joanne, her mouth dry. She could feel a pulse throbbing at her temple. She could hear her heart thumping, racing. Like heavy footsteps pounding after you on a dark and lonely street.

'Always figured him for a bit of a gangster. You know, acting tough, trying to be a gemme. . . .'

She could take no more. She stopped walking. She stood, arms rigid by her sides, staring straight ahead, seeing nothing. In her mind all the events of the past few days flashed by.

James halted. Looking at his sister the statue he suddenly felt quite awkward. She was like a zombie, glazed eyes fixed on an invisible object somewhere in the distance.

'Are you okay, Joanne?'

Like the clicking of the magician's fingers, the anxious note in his voice brought her out of the trance. She could contain her secret no longer. A hesitant trickle of words soon became a steady stream, flowing easily now as she recounted finding James's box, the money and the letter within. The stream swelled to a torrent as she rushed through her account of the meetings with Monty and Squeak. When she confessed her succumbing to temptation, actually removing James's hard-earned savings, the banks finally burst and her words were drowned out by her sobbing.

'I'm so sorry, James. I really am. . . .'

Instinctively, he put his arm around his not-so-little sister and drew her towards him. Conflicting emotions were waging war within him. He was angry, boy was he angry, at the thought of how close he had come to losing his chance to go to Italy. At the same time his heart went out to this mixed-up, chubby wee lassie who happened to be his sister. He understood how it felt to want something this badly. And he knew what it meant to feel isolated, rejected. For a long time he had missed his father. Desperately.

'It's okay, Jo-Jo, you didn't keep the money, did you? You only kind of borrowed it.'

'But I was all set to hand it over to Monty. Your money for a stupid bike.'

'The point is, Joanne, that you didn't go through with it.' James astonished himself with how reasonable he sounded. 'You knew it was wrong. You couldn't do it.'

Joanne did not recognise the brother speaking to her. He seemed considerate, understanding. Where was the old James who ridiculed her, who treated her with ill-concealed contempt?

'You're not annoyed?' she asked tentatively.

'I'm raging. I'm furious. I'm absolutely livid,' he admitted. 'But there's no point in taking it out on you, is there? You feel bad enough. I can't hurt you any more than you're hurting yourself.'

This new James was a strange creature. In spite of his school reports Joanne had never credited her brother with much intelligence. She had underestimated him.

'I'm sorry,' she found herself repeating, 'and I didn't mean to read your letter, honest. I couldn't help myself. . . .'

James squeezed her shoulder. Mentioning Dad was taboo in the house, a kind of tacit agreement. Only Jackie in her rages threw his name about, a weapon to hurl at Mum. He never allowed himself to make any reference to his absent father. They had been closest. He remembered his dad taking him to his first Rangers game, draping him in his own scarf, whirling him off his feet when McCoist scored. . . .

'It's alright, Joanne, I understand.' And the Big Brother did. 'We'll talk later, I promise. Let's find that mad rabbit first.'

United, the pair of them renewed their quest. The evening sun cast long shadows as they progressed up Lennon Street. They walked side by side now, indifferent to the sneers of any classmates they might encounter.

At the top of Lennon Street, where it met Ritchie Road, two groups of kids were playing. Half a dozen boys were involved in contesting the World Cup, using red traffic cones as makeshift goals. It was serious stuff. Only the occasional car driving through the 'stadium' interrupted the flow of the game. Adjacent to the pitch, where one might have expected a grandstand, some younger girls were playing 'beds', 'peever' as Nana called it.

Lennon Street had all been renovated recently. Everyone had been decanted, lock, stock and barrel, to vacant houses in the Glen while their homes were gutted. The kids in the area had had a field day rummaging amongst the skips looking for treasure. The scaffolding had provided hours of dangerous amusement. The watchman had been only too eager to add some spice to a new form of chases. Now, with the families installed in their spruce new accommodation, the girls (and not a few of the boys) appreciated how suitable the newly-laid paving stones were for pursuing this traditional pastime. A bit of chalk borrowed from the school and a flat stone or a tin lid and you were away.

'I'll take the boys and you question the girls.'

'Sexist,' hissed Joanne, although she wasn't quite sure what it meant. Miss Barrett who had taken the class for a few days when Miss Martin was on a course or something had tried to explain to them about women being treated unfairly. Like second-class citizens was one of the things she said. Joanne hadn't quite understood it all but had been impressed by Miss Barrett's forceful style. Oh, and you weren't supposed to call her Miss Barrett; it was Mizz.

To be honest, Joanne preferred talking to the girls anyway. In any event she had little success.

'Is there a reward for catching it?'

'Does it run after you when you shout on it?'

'Can we come and help you look for it?'

They asked most of the questions and the answer to each was 'No'.

James, having taken the opportunity to display his skills with an impromptu exhibition of 'keepy-uppy', soon rejoined her. He had had more luck.

'One of them says that his pal's dad saw a big white rabbit down the Plots on his way home from work.'

'Well, its worth a shot. Let's get cracking.'

The Plots lay in a little hollow at the foot of Saint Mungo's Hill. Originally these allotments had been set aside for the men who worked in the Kentigern Foundry. Twenty sections of land had been marked out, long, narrow carpets of top quality soil. In its heyday the Kentigern Allotment Society had organised fruit and vegetable competitions which drew gasps of wonder from the locals who discovered a veritable Garden of Eden on their grimy doorstep.

The Foundry had long gone, extinct like the greater part of Clydeside's heavy industry. Some nondescript warehouse complex now occupied the old site. Glasgow's giants had passed into mythology.

Less than half of the plots were still cultivated. Nobody seemed to know anyone who rented one. Yet these doughty gardeners fought to raise a few straggly rows of cabbages, a few pounds of potatoes, and some peas. Fought not only the elements, not only the voracious bugs, but also the human predators who envied them this tiny patch of tranquillity. Each plot was surrounded by wire fencing, each shed secured with a heavy padlock in a vain attempt to keep the vandals at bay.

As James and Joanne approached the Plots they glimpsed a solitary figure pressed against one of the huts. He was trying to prise up the hasp on the door, using a spade as a lever. It was Monty.

'Hey, what do you think you're doing?' yelled James, his earlier anger returning.

Coolly Monty propped the spade against the hut, straightened up, and faced the interlopers. 'Well, bless my soul, if it isn't Ratman and Dobbin, the gruesome twosome.' A smile spread across his face.

Even caught in the act, nothing seemed to faze him, thought Joanne.

'I'm sorry, madam, but, as you can see, I have no bicycles on offer at the present moment. My business partner is enjoying, if that's the right word, a well-deserved rest. The transport branch of our corporation is temporarily suspended.'

Joanne felt her face go red hot. At her side she sensed James tensing, a coil ready to spring.

'Aye, he's resting in Stobhill Hospital,' James growled, 'after trying to steal my money.' He was already halfway through a tear in the fence.

'An independent venture, I assure you,' continued Monty in the same mocking tone. 'I fully intend reprimanding him at the next visiting hour.'

James wasn't listening. He launched himself at Monty, clattering him against the side of the hut. The hut teetered. Joanne screamed.

James's pent-up rage exploded. His arms flailed, a windmill of punches, catching Monty on the shoulder and chest, but doing little damage. Deftly, Monty slipped under his opponent's onslaught, delivering a stinging open-handed slap to James's cheek as he evaded him.

'Stop!' Joanne bellowed. Both boys ignored her.

They were squaring up to one another. James had a wildness about him which frightened Joanne. Monty retained his usual grinning composure.

James telegraphed a swinging right-hand punch. Monty blocked it with his left forearm, stepped inside, and drove his right fist hard into James's stomach. He doubled up. Monty took a pace back as if admiring his handiwork.

'Stick to football, Jamesie,' he laughed. 'Leave the rough stuff to the big boys.'

James remained crouched, breathing hard. Joanne could still see the fire burning in his eyes. Suddenly he lunged forward, thrusting his shoulder into Monty's midriff, and throwing his arms around his waist. Monty staggered back a few steps before James's momentum dumped them both on the ground.

Thus entwined, the two bodies grappled, a shapeless maul where neither could strike a telling blow. Several rows of lettuce were crushed beneath them. Joanne stood bewildered at the stupidity of it all.

They rolled over, a mass of thrashing limbs. Fingers clawed at throats, elbows dug into ribs, knees pressed into muscle as each sought to gain an advantage. The rich dark soil clung to their clothing, obliterating any distinction. Only their voices provided a clue to their identity, as they maintained a barrage of threats and insults.

Joanne despaired. Where was the sensitive older brother of an hour ago? Writhing about in the mud like a wild animal. To prove what?

The fight was soon running out of steam. Neither boy could disengage the other. Their epic struggle had degenerated into a fumbling brawl. Both were panting from their exertions. Soon they wouldn't have sufficient breath to declare an honourable draw. They clasped one another, unable to win, unwilling to lose. If only the bell would signal the end of the contest.

Relief was at hand. Three plots down a figure appeared, slinking between the rows of carrots. He shuffled along, paused, twitched his nose in the direction of the melee, then turned tail, a lovely white bob, and scuttled off towards the far end of the Plots.

Joanne tugged frantically at what she hoped was James's sleeve. 'It's Moby! Over there! Look!'

James twisted his head round in time to snatch a fleeting glimpse of his runaway pet. With a final effort he shoved himself off his enemy, flopping onto his back to regain his breath. Monty briefly considered clipping his foe on the head one last time but he had no wish to renew hostilities. He too sank down in the dirt.

'Satisfied?' demanded Joanne. 'Two big tough guys. Playing at mud pies. Meanwhile Moby is still running about loose. Come on, get up, you, and let's get after him.'

Slowly James dragged himself to his feet. He glared at Monty who had made himself comfortable amid the vegetables. He lay with his hands under his head as if he were relaxing on the beach. His grin had returned.

'Better chase after your little bunny rabbit, Jamesie. It will be dark soon and you know your mummy will be worried if you're not tucked up in bed.'

Joanne pulled her brother away. She wanted to say something cutting to Monty, to put him in his place, but she didn't have the words. She pushed James ahead of her, using her weight and his exhaustion to propel him along the path. James muttered a string of curses under his breath.

'Oh, children,' Monty called, as they reached the end of the allotments, 'I'll keep an eagle eye out for Peter Rabbit. I'm extremely fond of our lapine friends. Especially with a nice rich sauce.'

Joanne shuddered as Monty's cackling laugh died away.

CHAPTER

Was that a brass band striking up? Could that possibly be fireworks exploding in kaleidoscopic patterns overhead? Did that low rumble herald the first discharge of a twenty-one gun salute?

No. Someone's ghetto-blaster was turned up to the max. The sunshine and the rain were engaged in a tug of war. Paladin Street juddered under the weight of the early morning traffic.

Some events in your life, thought Joanne, should be marked in a special way, like birthdays. Leaving primary school was such an occasion.

Not that she was glad to see the back of Wee Northwood, mind you. She had enjoyed her time there. She'd made some good friends. Well, there was Sara! She'd got on famously with all her teachers. Except old Clarke of the diamond knuckle dusters. She'd coped easily with the work. Okay, maybe she hadn't exactly excelled in Mr. Craig's daily torture, sorry, P.E., sessions.

Nor was she particularly overjoyed at the prospect

of going up to the Big School. No longer would she be at the top of the school. Now she was starting all over again, the youngest.

Oh, she had heard the horror stories. Head shoved down toilets. Chased by the Second Years. Hand over your tuck money! James had told her how exaggerated these alarming tales were. Anyway, she was sure that her new Big Brother would look out for her.

The Secondary held few fears, but neither was it an irresistible attraction.

The building itself was hardly inspiring. If I collected a dozen cornflake boxes, stuck them together, cut out windows, and then painted the cardboard grey, I'd have a fair replica of Big Northwood. What would I do for the cracked walls and the peeling paint, the damp ceilings and the draughty corridors?

And then there was the Fence. The latest design feature was a ten-foot-high fence enclosing the school. To keep the Vandals from desecrating the hallowed halls of education.

'To keep us in,' insisted James. 'It's Barlinnie for beginners. Bar-L High.'

Joanne allowed herself a smile as she recalled her brother's joke. To be honest, she and Sara had enjoyed the two days they had spent visiting the Big School.

What had Miss Martin called it? A 'Familiarisation Exercise'?

They had been whisked round by a big girl in the Sixth Year, Suzanne, who, Pied Piper fashion, led the class through a maze of corridors and stairways from one subject to the next. Most of it was new, exciting but confusing. 'Home Ecies,' 'Techi', Science, French.

Sara was waiting as usual at Beechwood. She looks a bit agitated, thought Joanne, but decided to wait until her friend chose to tell her what was troubling her. That was the best approach with Sara.

'What subject did you like best when we went up to Big Northwood?' she asked, to fill the silence.

Sara walked along, staring steadfastly at her feet. 'I don't know. None of them. All of them. . . .'

This vagueness was unsatisfactory. 'Come on, Sara, there must be one you're looking forward to. What about Technical? That Mr. Sawyer was nice. And her in Art, Mrs. Whistler, was a good laugh.'

The girls in the class had all agreed that Mr. Sawyer was indeed the nicest of the teachers on show. Certainly the nicest looking. Unlike Mr. Brock in Science. The Badger, James called him. More like a toad with his thick neck and bulging eyes. Joanne hadn't taken to him at all. Didn't seem to like kids. It wasn't anything he said in that slow, monotonous voice of his. More just a kind of feeling that they were getting in the way of his precious lesson.

'I really enjoyed Computing,' Joanne babbled on. 'Mr. Finch says we can finish off our project when we come to Secondary.'

Sara still didn't respond. Her shoes held a fascination.

'Stop a minute,' Joanne commanded. 'What's the matter? You look as though somebody's stolen your doughnut.'

Her pal smiled at Joanne's turn of phrase. 'The loss of a cake is more likely to upset you than me.'

'Are you implying, Miss Devlin, Miss Skin-and-Bone, Miss Skeleton, that I am overweight, plump, fat!' Joanne succeeded in capturing just the correct note of comic indignation.

Sara giggled. Surveying her friend she was forced to admit that she appeared to have shed a few pounds in the last few weeks.

'Alright I take it back. You look as if someone just swiped your computer. Not that you with all your genius actually need one.'

'You're not so thick yourself, Joanne McCallum. . . .'

'Gordon,' corrected Joanne. 'Come on, spill the beans. What's bugging you?'

'I'm scared,' confided Sara, her voice little more

than a whisper. She was inspecting her laces again. The sun glinted off her spectacles.

'Scared?' repeated Joanne. 'Scared of what? Has Monty been bothering you?' The boy with the bad skin and the big vocabulary hadn't been much in evidence recently. Gone to ground somewhere. Planning his next big job.

'Monty doesn't scare me. Maybe just a bit . . .' Sara trailed off. Joanne could see her pal collecting herself, preparing to unload her burden, trusting her to help shoulder it.

'It's going to a new school, being thrown in with new people. Everyone says the work is far harder too.'

'Don't talk nonsense, Sara. Are you going to waste the summer holidays worrying about going to Big Northwood? I'll be there, you bampot. And let's face it, any new people would be an improvement on the likes of Colin McBain and Angela McInnes. And as for the work! You're the school's resident brainbox. If you can't do it what hope is there for the rest of us, eh?'

A bit over the top, Joanne. Sara was painfully shy, easily embarrassed, and even more easily hurt. She would have to take her under her wing. Old Mother Joanne. Supposing they managed to land up in the same registration class. . . .

'Right, enough of this rubbish. We've got a disco waiting for us. Let's get down on it. Let's boogie!'

Sara, still not quite reassured, grinned at her friend's ridiculous choice of words. They set off for Wee Northwood for the last time, each concealing a sense of dread. For obvious reasons they both detested discos.

The school had made a huge effort to ensure the final term remained fixed forever in the minds of Primary 7. They had visited Glasgow's Glasgow, rambled round Kelburne Country Park, competed in a triangular Fun Day with the other feeder schools, and spent a day at Butlins. Okay, the exhibition was a wee bit boring, it had rained cats and dogs at Kelburne, they had won the wooden spoon on the Fun Day, and half the class had spewed all over the bus on the way home from Ayr, but it still seemed like Christmas in June.

The disco maintained this standard of excellence. Nobody asked Joanne or Sara to dance. They would have refused in any case. The boys had succeeded in ripping most of the decorations from the walls. Two weeks' wasted effort. And Mr. Craig played only last month's hit records. 'Top of the Pops'? Forget it!

At least the food was good. Or it would have been if Joanne had permitted herself to taste any of the mouth-watering cakes on offer. Sara watched in admiration.

At a signal from Miss Martin, Mr. Craig lifted the

needle off the record currently emptying the dancefloor. Another scratch. Someone at the back of the assembly hall switched on the main lights.

'Well, boys and girls, I apologise for interrupting your fun. I'm glad to see you all having such a good time . . .'

Colin McBain blew what was to be his ultimate raspberry in primary school. Miss Martin chose to ignore Colin's customary display of wit.

'. . . but I have an important announcement to make.'

There was a slight stirring of interest.

'As you know, earlier this month one of our local shops, "Deals on Wheels", ran a competition for the best essay on the topic of cycling.'

Sara nudged Joanne. Both girls held their breath. Joanne didn't dare hope. It would be a greater disappointment if another person in the class, Angela McInnes say, won the bike.

'I am delighted to announce that one of our Primary Sevens . . .'

Get on with it!

'. . . in the face of fierce competition from pupils in Allandale and Muirhead . . .'

Hisses and boos.

'. . . has been awarded first prize in this contest.'

Joanne dug her nails into the palms of her hands. Her throat was like sandpaper.

'I am pleased to introduce Mr. Ross, owner of the shop, who will announce the winner and present the prize. Mr. Ross!'

Miss Martin and the other teachers in attendance attempted to prompt a round of applause. Only the adults clapped.

From the rear of the hall a small figure advanced on the stage, bounded up the steps and shook hands with Miss Martin. He bore little resemblance to the harlequin who capered about the cycle shop. A smart navy blue suit had replaced the dazzling vest and shorts. He even wore real shoes. When he focussed those twinkling eyes on the patient multitude, however, there was no mistaking the ebullient Jockey Ross.

Were those laughing eyes settling on her?

'Hello, boys and girls, and thank you Miss Martin for welcoming me to your school. I know you all want to get on with your jigging. Who wants to hear an old fogey blithering on? So let me get on with the presentation.

'First of all I've got to say that I was really impressed with all the entries submitted. Did your teacher stand over you and make you dot all the i's and cross all the t's? And the big words! I tell you I had to buy a dictionary to help me understand half of what you were saying.'

Some polite laughter.

'There were loads of great stories sent in. I wish I could give all of you a prize, but I'd be bankrupt. There can only be one winner. A bit like the road races I used to ride in.

'It was a very difficult decision. Some stories were thrilling, others were clever, a few were a wee bit sad. In the end I picked the one I thought wrote best about how it felt to be up on a bike, wheeching along the country roads. I know that feeling well. Have done since I was your age.

'I'm not going to read the winning entry out. Miss Martin has arranged for the "Argus" to print it so everyone can have a read of it. And as you can see I've not got the bike hidden up my juke. The winner'll have to come to the shop and pick out their own special bicycle.

'So can I ask the lucky person to step up here and get a big cheer from their classmates . . . Joanne Gordon of 7A!'

In a trance Joanne made her way forward. The crowd parted like the Red Sea. Over-enthusiastic hands slapped her on the back. And this time there was a spontaneous round of applause.

Later on Sara informed her that her face had been

glowing like a Christmas tree. Radiant was the term she used. If the old Joanne had come across a gingerbread house in the middle of the park she couldn't have been any happier.

Jockey grabbed her hand and shook it warmly. He held onto it, all the time chatting away to her in that animated fashion of his. Joanne didn't take in a single word. She wanted to laugh and sing and dance and turn cartwheels all at the same time. And ride a bike round and round the hall.

A man with a camera appeared from nowhere, popping off flashbulbs in her face. Her and Jockey. Her and Miss Martin. The three of them together. And any kid who could get in the photo.

Another signal. The lights dimmed. The music blasted out. Ceremony over.

'Tomorrow. First thing tomorrow, young yin, at the shop. We'll make a cyclist out of you yet.'

Then he was gone. Sara guided her friend to a seat in the corner where Joanne could drift away into her dreams.

Everybody deserves one good day.

CHAPTER

As far as the Gordon family was concerned this was it. Joanne rushed home at midday, bursting to tell her wonderful news. Ian was seated at the kitchen table. Margaret Gordon sat across from him, the picture of contentment. Steven lay asleep in the next room.

Ian was owed a few days and on the spur of the moment had travelled down from Aberdeen to be with his wife. Soon, he knew, he would chuck the rigs and return to Glasgow for good. He missed Margaret. No amount of money could compensate for not being with her.

Joanne had no time to waste on greetings. Ian would get a hug later. She launched straight into the story of her marvellous success. If there was a category in 'The Guinness Book of Records' for being able to speak quickly she must be a contender. Later that night Ian would liken her to an Olympic long jumper.

'She set off fast, gathered speed on the run-up, hit the board smack on, and took off into the air.'

'And she hasn't landed yet,' her mother added. 'I just hope that she doesn't come down to earth with a bang.'

Joanne was still as high as a kite throughout lunch. Between spoonfuls of yoghurt she babbled on about the bike, her bike, and the various runs which she planned to undertake with Sara. Margaret and Ian realised that anything they might have to say to one another would have to be postponed. They contented themselves with holding hands across the table.

Only after she had gulped down a glass of milk and was about to sink her teeth into a firm green apple did it dawn on Joanne that James was not present at the meal.

'Where's James? I can't wait to tell him.'

'James? Your brother James? You remember him then?'

Her mother's quietly sarcastic tone made Joanne feel a bit sheepish.

'And here I was thinking that this family consisted of me, Ian, you and a bicycle yet to be christened.'

Joanne screwed up her eyes and made a face.

'It's his big day too, you know,' Margaret chided gently.

'Oh, his Cup Final! I forgot. Well, I didn't forget . . . It was just with the bike . . .' Joanne felt a twinge of guilt at her selfishness.

'We thought we might all take a run up to the park to watch,' said Ian. 'Lend a bit of support. Watch the maestro in action.'

Joanne nodded with genuine enthusiasm. A Gordon family outing. She would push the pram.

Her mother placed a sheet of notepaper with a crest at the top on Joanne's table-mat. The familiar handwriting jolted her. A reply from her dad.

Margaret ran water into a basin while Ian cleared the table, their industry allowing Joanne some privacy to read her letter. The words danced in front of her eyes. Something about a new job. The Rob Roy and Trossachs something or other. Missing her. And Jackie and James of course. Inviting her to spend a week with him during the summer.

'He's asked if I can go. . . .'

'I know. Your letter was inside one he sent to me.' Margaret's voice was strained. Her first reaction had been to rip up both letters. Perhaps if Ian hadn't arrived, if he hadn't talked it over with her in that quiet sensible way of his, the letters would be so many scraps at the foot of the bin.

Joanne glanced from her mother to Ian. He gave her a comforting smile.

'I don't want to go.'

'Don't be daft. Of course you want to go. He is your dad, after all. He still loves you. And you love him.' Margaret Gordon forced the words out. 'Besides James is off to Italy and Jackie and Sean are waltzing off as well. If we can get shot of you Ian, the baby and me can have a nice quiet time to ourselves, can't we, Ian?' A tear.

'Aye,' he agreed, 'we deserve a break from you three, a chance to have the run of the place.' He playfully patted his wife's bottom.

'In his letter to me he says its alright to bring a friend with you if you want. Plenty of room apparently. Seems to have landed on his feet this time.' She couldn't keep the note of bitterness out of her voice. 'So I took the liberty of phoning Mrs. Devlin to ask if Sara was allowed to go with you.'

The glow returned to Joanne's face.

'She'll have to discuss it with her husband, she says, but it looks promising.'

Joanne knew big, cuddly George Devlin would agree as long as everything was arranged properly. He would convince his wife that they needed to let Sara off the leash a bit. She couldn't be wrapped in cotton wool forever.

Margaret Gordon watched her daughter relaxing into the idea. She knew she had kept one thing back. John had met someone. Evelyn. From the sound of things it was pretty serious. Oh well, he could explain all that when Joanne arrived.

James wore a canary yellow jersey with a black number eight printed on the back, black shorts, and yellow socks with two thin black bands at the top. He was playing for the school, her school now. In the past Joanne had frequently been confused by the variety of strips which filled the wash-basket.

Northwood Secondary played in yellow and black, Northwood Boys' Club turned out in blue and yellow, sorry, royal and gold, while the B.B. wore a horrible ensemble of purple and silver. She hadn't as yet come to terms with the away strips!

Ian had been proved correct. James was a maestro. Even Joanne with her scant knowledge of the game could see that he was dominating the game. Football seemed to provide exactly the right arena for his character. He strutted about the field, directing his team-mates, urging them on. There was a cockiness to his play, almost a lavish extravagance about the manner in which he glided past opponents, caressing the ball with the outside of his boot, before stroking it accurately to one of his team. He was in his element.

The match itself was no contest. Northwood were three goals ahead with only a few minutes remaining. James had scored the second goal raising his arms aloft as the ball settled in the back of the net.

Steven was fretting. Joanne wheeled the pram away from the pitch towards the pond, secretly glad to escape. Away from people she sang softly to her baby brother.

'You should be on the stage,' a voice behind her said. Without turning, the ever-present mockery in the voice told her it was Monty.

'I know. There's one leaving in five minutes.' She stopped now to confront her old adversary. She considered him an enemy, but he hadn't in fact done anything to her. He annoyed her. A waste.

'I've a present for you,' he said. The spots on his face didn't seem so angry today. His grin was as wide as ever. For the first time Joanne noticed that the smile never reached his eyes.

'A present?' He was empty-handed and there was no place to conceal a gift of any size. He was dressed in denims and a T-shirt. The shirt bore the logo of some heavy metal group. A skull with flames shooting from its eyes.

'Let me try again in words of one syllable,' Monty intoned. 'I - have - a - gift - for - you.'

'What gift?'

'What is this? Twenty Questions? I'll give you a clue. It has big ears . . . No it's not an elephant!'

'Moby! Where is he?' Joanne swivelled her head to see if she could locate a box or something which might contain the rabbit. Nothing.

'He awaits your return. I conducted him, suitably

housed, naturally, to your close but answer came there none. So I deposited him, reluctant to carry the beast further.'

A terrifying image entered Joanne's head. Old Granny Stewart's cats! Rabbit fur on the stairs!

'The cats will tear him apart!'

'What, those scabby moggies belonging to the old witch down below you? Her familiars? I sensed their delicate aroma as soon as I set foot in the close. Never fear. I constructed a solid fortress from old bricks in your washhouse and secured the said rabbit within.'

Relief swept through Joanne, followed by suspicion.

'I suppose you're expecting a reward. A few bob for your trouble.'

The boy looked aggrieved. How could she think so ill of him?

'No reward. I see it as a debt of honour. If my comrade had not ventured into your washhouse, for whatever purpose, the bunny would never have escaped to taste the freedom of the countryside that is Northwood.'

For the umpteenth time Joanne felt exasperated at the contradictory nature of this boy. An obviously intelligent mind devoted to squandering his talents. She stammered out a thanks but Monty was already striding out towards the pitch.

The wind taken out of her sails, she decided to drop the anchor. She plumped herself down on a bench, all the while maintaining a soothing rocking motion of the pram. She glanced once more in the direction of the game.

The ball was hastily booted off the park by a desperate defender. She watched as Monty casually trapped it with his left foot and in the same flowing movement flicked it deftly into the hands of the player dispatched to retrieve it.

Any further spectating was made impossible as a pair of hands snaked round from behind and covered her eyes.

'Guess who?'

'Jackie!'

The hands were lifted. Vision was restored. Jackie came and joined her on the bench.

'What are you doing here? Shouldn't you still be at work?'

'Left early, didn't I? Took the afternoon off. Went with Sean to. . . .'

'Jacqueline Gordon, why are you not at work? Are you not well? Did Mrs. Imrie send you home?' The game over, victory achieved, Ian and Margaret had come in search of their offspring.

'I've got a surprise for you,' Jackie began. 'Sean and me have got engaged.'

And, indeed, a large ring encrusted with what might have been diamonds flashed on her left hand.

A look passed between Margaret and Ian. Joanne could not determine its significance. A second, inquiring, look passed between mother and newly affianced daughter. There would be much to discuss later.

Joanne discharged Steven into Ian's care. The family headed over to see the trophy being presented.

Joanne wondered whether if she took a stroll down Paladin Street Jockey might still be in his shop. . . .